AFTER Dusk

LORIE O'CLARE

ELLORA'S CAVE
ROMANTICA PUBLISHING

What the critics are saying...

ကာ

5 Stars! "Ms.O'Clare knows how to build heart stopping scenes that will have you speculating throughout the entire book all the while experiencing luscious, passionate sexual encounters between Emily and the hero of the story, Rafe."

~ *Erotic Escapades*

5 Cups! "This book is absolutely fabulous. It was almost like watching a movie unfold in front of me." ~ *Coffee Time Romance*

5 Stars! "Score one for Ms. O'Clare who has taken a suspenseful thriller and woven it with a sensual love story."

~ *Just Erotic Romance Reviews*

5 Stars! "After Dusk in many ways is a character study of a psychotic murderer. Lorie's method of gradually revealing clues keeps the tension and excitement high. Rafe and Emily really came alive under Lorie's pen. The love scenes were hot and exquisite." ~ *ECataRomance*

5 Stars! "Lorie O'Clare's characters so often have such depth that you'd expect them to jump off the page and move in next to you. This is how well-written this cast is in *After Dusk.*" ~ *Fallen Angels Reviews*

An Ellora's Cave Romantica Publication

www.ellorascave.com

After Dusk

ISBN 1419955454, 9781419955457
Edited by Sue-Ellen Gower.
Cover art by Syneca.

This book printed in the U.S.A. by Jasmine–Jade Enterprises, LLC.

Electronic book Publication December 2005
Trade paperback Publication December 2006

Excerpt from *Caught!* Copyright © Lorie O'Clare 2005

Also by Lorie O'Clare

ജ

About the Author

ဆာ

All my life, I've wondered at how people fall into the routines of life. The paths we travel seemed to be well-trodden by society. We go to school, fall in love, find a line of work (and hope and pray it is one we like), have children and do our best to mold them into good people who will travel the same path. This is the path so commonly referred to as the "real world".

The characters in my books are destined to stray down a different path other than the one society suggests. Each story leads the reader into a world altered slightly from the one they know. For me, this is what good fiction is about, an opportunity to escape from the daily grind and wander down someone else's path.

Lorie O'Clare lives in Kansas with her three sons.

Lorie welcomes comments from readers. You can find her website and email address on her author bio page at www.ellorascave.com.

Tell Us What You Think
We appreciate hearing reader opinions about our books. You can email us at Comments@EllorasCave.com.

AFTER DUSK

&

Dedication

ౠ

Personally, I don't like the dark shadows at night. You'll never get me to sit down and watch a scary movie with you. But I wanted to try something that I'd never done before. And I had some inspiration.

A very, very long time ago – we won't go into how many years ago – a dear friend and critique partner let me read a scene she wrote. It terrified me, which made me mad. I told her that I hated being scared. She knew that about me. Yet she sent the scene to me anyway, not telling me that it would be scary, gross, disturbing. To this day, I still see that scene in my head.

That friend went on to become a best selling erotic romance writer. What she showed me a long time ago, works in every genre. If you move the reader, grab hold of them and twist their emotions then you've got them – whether they are sexual emotions, or being scared of the dark.

We love sex. We love violence, whether we like to admit it or not. When something terrible happens, we want the details, to know what happened. Mix those two together, and you have one of the most enticing genres on the market – an erotic thriller!

With this story, all of your emotions will be drawn out. You will hate, cry, get excited, turned on, and scream with delight – and fear – over some of the scenes in this book. It is an incredible ride, one that moved me greatly writing it, and one that I hope leaves you feeling exhilarated.

Thank you Shadoe, for the bats. And I'm still waiting for your erotic thriller!

Trademarks Acknowledgement

The author acknowledges the trademarked status and trademark owners of the following wordmarks mentioned in this work of fiction:

Dumpster: Dempster Brothers, Inc.

eBay: eBay Inc.

FedEx: Federal Express Corporation

Firebird: General Motors Corporation

Taurus: Ford Motor Company

UPS: United Parcel Service of America, Inc.

Prologue

೫

"Are you sure we're safe here?" Closing her car door, she stared at the glow of the city lights against the dark horizon.

"We're safe." He wrapped his arms around her, turning her around and pushing her against the hood of the car.

Solid muscle was like steel everywhere he touched her. God. There wasn't an ounce of fat on him anywhere.

"There's something about you," he said, his voice deep, husky, turning her on. "Maybe it's that you're not like all the young girls on campus."

"I'm not old," she said, laughing, loving his firm grip when he pinned her against the warm hood of his car.

"Oh no. You know I didn't mean it like that." He pressed his erection against her ass, a steel beam with promises that made her insides swell.

"There's something about you too," she whispered, her heart pounding against metal. "Fast and confident. Your sex drive matching mine."

"Exactly. That's what I meant. God. I need to fuck you."

"What's keeping you?" She wiggled her ass against his, her insides burning with need as he groaned above her.

"Shit," he groaned.

He worked at his jeans, desperately trying to free his cock while his knuckles rubbed against her ass, her cunt, freeing her juices, driving her nuts with anticipation.

"God. Hurry. I need you inside me." She brushed hair from her face, glancing around at the trees that partially hid them from the highway.

Crickets sang, a cool breeze wrapped around her. The danger of the moment, fucking outside where anyone could walk up on them, made her pussy swell. She'd had her eyes on this guy all semester. And now, finally, she would have him.

Ever since her divorce, dealing with returning to school, negotiating child custody, balancing studying with her job— damn it, she deserved this.

His fingers shook as he reached up under her skirt, pulling her panties down so that they trapped her legs together. And then she felt him. That hard, swollen cock pressing against her pulsing cunt. Unable to spread her legs for him, she arched her back, dying to have him slam that thing deep inside her.

"Fuck me. Now," she ordered, knowing she would die if he didn't relieve the ache soon.

"God. I love older women. You know what you want."

And he obeyed. Pushing his cock inside her, the swollen soft head covering his rock hardness, he filled her, spread her open, stroked her pussy wall as he entered her. Scraping her fingers over his hood, she cried out, her dam of frustration breaking instantly as he satisfied a need that had grown over the months.

"More. Faster. Harder." She looked over her shoulder, barely able to see him, ordering him to take care of her.

"Yes, ma'am," he said, a chuckle in his tone.

Quickly picking up the pace, he pounded her cunt, bringing her to orgasm quickly as he stroked her, quenching desires that had been put on hold for months.

Closing her eyes, she enjoyed the moment, experiencing complete satisfaction with his large cock. When she felt him swell, knew he was about to explode, he pulled out, spilling his hot cum over her ass.

"God, that looks good." His voice was raspy. "Hold on. I'll find something to wipe you off."

She relaxed against the car hood, her pussy still throbbing. He hadn't lasted long. She'd take more of him. But youth had its downfalls. There weren't any complaints though. It had been better sex than she'd had in a while. Hell. It had been the only sex she'd had in a while.

A twig snapped behind her and she opened her eyes lazily. Something hard pressed against her soaked pussy and then entered her, feeling different than his cock somehow. Had he brought toys?

Looking over her shoulder, she saw his dark shadow but at the same time felt a nasty stab in the middle of her back. Pain flooded through her with more severity than she'd ever experienced in her life, immobilizing her, making it impossible to lift her head.

Something thrust deep inside her, but the pain that spread through her made it impossible for her to focus on it.

"So you like the young ones?" The voice didn't make sense.

Or maybe that it didn't sound right.

"They think you're so much better, but they're wrong." The voice was all wrong, like a screaming whisper.

Trying desperately to turn, to look behind her, the hood of the car seemed to slide out from underneath her. No matter what she did, she couldn't control her actions. Her body didn't want to cooperate. It was darker than it had been a moment before as she fell backwards, staring up at the shadow of a figure above her. It was the last thing she saw before her world went black.

Chapter One

ာ

"Your syllabus will show you when assignments are due and what needs to be read for each class. We'll move at an accelerated pace, so if you don't think you can keep up, you have until Friday to drop the class." Professor Jenkins looked over his glasses at the class.

Emily stared at the papers on her desk, shifting in the uncomfortable wooden chair. The guy sitting next to her snored quietly. Flipping through the stapled papers, she looked at the assignment due for the next class. She frowned, looking up at the professor.

His bushy gray hair looked like it hadn't seen a brush in years. Nibbling on the tip of her pen, she slowly raised her hand.

"Yes…" Professor Jenkins frowned at her.

Taking her pen from her mouth she smiled. "Emily. Emily Rothmeier."

The professor humphed, scowling further. "You have a question?"

"Yes. Yes, I do. The syllabus says you want us to read one hundred pages by Friday. That's two days from now."

Professor Jenkins stared at her, obviously not following her line of thinking.

She cleared her throat, ignoring the many eyes that now stared at her. Next time she would sit in the front row so she couldn't see everyone else.

"That's a lot of reading. And this isn't my only class. I've got a day job."

Several people around her snickered. Others simply began organizing their books. The professor looked at her as if she were on drugs. Then he let his gaze scan the class.

"Any other questions? If not, we'll see you on Friday." Not to mention he had the nerve to refer to himself in the third person.

Emily let out a frustrated sigh. Maybe she was too old to be returning to college, or in her case, giving college a try for the first time. But damn it, there had to be more to life than waiting tables until her knees gave out.

Everyone quickly left the classroom, leaving her to organize her papers into her backpack. The thing weighed half a ton when she threw it over her shoulder. Now for the long trek across campus to her car.

The professor gathered his papers and turned to leave.

"You know, I didn't mean to insult you," she told him, staring at the older man who looked no different than men she'd waited on for years. "Maybe you could tell me how a person is supposed to work and go to college."

The professor might be older, but he wasn't dead. His gaze dropped to her oversized breasts, breasts she'd been cursed with since the eighth grade. She wanted to wave at the man and say, *hey, I'm up here.*

"Miss…umm…I'm sorry, what was your name again?"

Maybe he'd forget she'd be the one turning in the poorly done assignment and give her a good grade. She sighed, bringing his attention back to her face.

"Emily Rothmeier," she told him.

"Yes. Emily. We'll have a lecture over the material on Friday. If the class is too hard for you, feel free to drop it."

"You sound like you want me to drop it?" If this was supposed to be a place of higher education, Professor Jenkins sure wasn't encouraging her.

"The first week is when we weed out those who think American Literature is an easy A." Again he turned for the door.

"Look, Professor. No one has ever handed me anything on a silver platter. I'll have your one hundred pages read by Friday." And it better be a damned good lecture, she wanted to add but instead marched past him out of the classroom.

Damn it. There was nothing worse than someone implying she was stupid. She'd had enough of that living in Auburn, Nebraska. Moving to Kansas City, enrolling in the West Hills Junior College, had been a major change in life for her. But she did it so she could make something out of her life. No absentminded professor was going to talk down to her.

A handful of students lingered in the hall, most of them barely looking old enough to drink.

"Way to tell off old Jenkins," a strapping jock-type told her, falling into pace alongside her as she headed down the hallway.

"Obviously it did a lot of good."

Several others waited at the elevator. Emily noticed the door for the stairs and headed for it. The jock followed her.

"Maybe we could get together for a beer," he said, his voice echoing somewhat in the narrow stairwell.

It was darker too, the light fading when the heavy door clanged shut behind them. Her tennis shoes padded on the stairs while his boots stomped on each step right behind her.

Halfway down the staircase, someone opened the door above, descending behind them on the stairs. Making a note not to do the stairs again at night, Emily ignored the uncomfortable sensation that rushed through her. She was on campus with hundreds of people nearby somewhere. She was perfectly safe.

"Well, how about it?" the jock asked when she didn't say anything. "Older women have always turned me on."

She pulled the door open at the bottom of the stairs, her discomfort quickly replaced with anger.

"Older women?" She looked up at the muscular boy. He wasn't bad-looking, obviously just not gifted in the intelligence department. "I am not an older woman."

He shrugged and smiled as if that were apology enough and followed her to the glass doors that led outside the building. She stopped when she hit the steps leading to the long sidewalk and grassy yard, which at the moment didn't have enough light. No way was this horny child following her to her car.

His gaze dropped to her breasts and she adjusted her backpack so that she clutched it to her front.

"No offense," he said, offering her a boyish grin. His blond hair was cut short and his teeth were perfect. He'd have no problem fucking half the student body. "How about the beer?"

"I'm not interested." She returned the grin and then headed down the steps.

If she went the entire semester without getting laid, she wouldn't give in to this overgrown hormone.

She'd made it to the bottom before he hurried after her.

"Guess I'll see you in class on Friday then." His grin had faded. More than likely he didn't hear no too often. "Be careful walking in the dark."

With that he headed off across the lawn, leaving her alone out front of the building. Several other students came out of the front of the building, probably those who'd taken the elevator.

"I liked the way you gave it to old Professor Jenkins," a scrawny boy, taller than her but skinny enough to be blown over by a good wind, said with a toothy smile.

The small group around him chimed in their agreement.

"I guess I just need to get accustomed to the workload," Emily said with a shrug, although she smiled at the young people.

Never in a million years would she have thought of herself standing on a campus discussing classes with other students.

"Jenkins thinks the world revolves around his classes." A heavy-set girl shrugged then rolled her eyes.

"Maybe you'd like to join us to study sometime," the tall skinny kid said, immediately blushing.

"I'd like that." Emily smiled reassuringly, trying to ease his obvious nervousness over the suggestion.

"That would be so cool." The heavy-set girl gave the boy next to her an odd look but then focused on Emily. "We'd love the opinion of an older woman. You're probably really smart."

Getting accustomed to being called older would take some time. She told them to let her know when a good time would be and then said her goodbyes.

Hurrying down the long sidewalk toward the street, the damp night air still carried warmth from the day. Tall trees cast dark shadows reminding her of home.

Kansas City, Missouri, wasn't all that different from Auburn, Nebraska, other than the fact that it was a good twenty times larger. There was no way she'd ever get accustomed to the traffic. But the weather was about the same.

Adjusting her backpack and then tugging on her tank top, she picked up her pace, crossing the street and heading toward the parking lot.

A long flight of stairs made it easier to head down the hilly incline toward the paved lot below. Whoever said this part of the country was flat had never been on this campus. If anything, her legs would tone up going to school.

Scattered streetlights threw odd shadows and made it hard to tell if small bordering trees were people or not. A sense of unease settled through her. It would take a while to get accustomed to being out at night like this. Back home, by dark she was always settled in for the evening.

Which was why she'd moved here. She had no life.

Voices distracted her and she scanned the parking lot, noticing a couple standing on the other side of an isolated car at the far end of the lot. Keeping her head down, she offered them their privacy and hurried toward her car. They were far enough away they wouldn't notice her.

Swinging her backpack around her shoulder, she unzipped the front pocket and fished for her keys.

A shrill scream made her stumble over her own feet, and she dropped her keys. Looking around frantically, she no longer saw the couple. There was one figure though, and it ran from the parking lot, darting up the side of the hill with a lot more ease than she could have put into it.

Shaking so hard her backpack slid from her shoulder, she fought the straps that suddenly confined her arm. The scream echoed in her head. Her keys were somewhere on the ground around her. Her backpack fell, the contents of the unzipped pouch spilling onto the blacktop as she looked frantically for her keys.

"Damn it." Dropping to her knees, she searched the ground, but at the same time her attention was distracted as she continually looked up, scanning the darkness around her.

Her heart pounded so hard that a herd of elephants could have come up behind her and she wouldn't have heard it.

"Shit," she hissed, scraping her knuckles on the blacktop when she scooped up her keys.

Somehow finding everything that had spilled out of her backpack, she stood, cursing her wobbly legs and hurrying to her car. Her heart raced almost as quickly as her hand shook. People didn't just scream for the heck of it. Getting the damned key in the little hole in the dark seemed impossible.

Her heart about exploded through her rib cage when footsteps and voices sounded in the distance. God. Now she knew why she was always in her nightgown, cuddled in front of her TV by dark every night. What kind of fool did she think she was enrolling in night classes?

"The only difference with the dark is that the sun is gone," she mumbled to herself, repeating what her mother had told her repeatedly as a child.

Glancing over her shoulder, she took a long slow breath, fighting to calm her nerves as she searched the parking lot. Several students had descended the stairs, chatting easily as they walked to their cars.

It was a large campus, with people everywhere. The students heading toward her didn't act as if anything were out of the ordinary. Maybe she'd overreacted. The shriek she'd heard could have been someone just goofing around. Maybe students in big cities did just scream for the heck of it.

Her key slid easily into her car door keyhole and light flooded her personal space when she opened her door. Two boys, and she didn't use the term lightly—they didn't look old enough to even drink—walked toward her, continuing with their conversation about some video game. Backpacks bounced against their backs as they continued past her without a glance in her direction.

One more look around the parking lot didn't help calm her. She focused on where she'd seen the couple earlier. Looking at the hill that the man had bounded up, it was a direct line away from where the couple had been standing.

And damn it, she had heard a woman scream.

Scowling for having watched way too many episodes of *Murder She Wrote*, Emily slid into her driver's seat and started her engine. A good detective would chase that person up the hill, pull off feats a professional gymnast would be proud of and have the case solved before the police arrived. Investigating crimes had its appeal in her imagination. Catching the bad guy single-handed, shrugging off all praise. But in real life... Hell, she was scared of the dark. And everyone knew that all detectives spent most of their time wandering around alone at night.

With her backpack in the seat next to her, she headed out of the parking lot, doing her best to put it all out of her mind. She had way too much homework to be thinking about anything else.

All that greeted her when she let herself into the small apartment she'd leased just two weeks ago were stacks of boxes. It had taken a week to move down here from Auburn, and then this past week she'd pulled double-shifts in order to give herself a running start with decent paychecks.

Finding time to make this place her new home, handle her new job and keep up with her studies was going to be next to impossible. After just one night of classes, she already was overwhelmed.

"How do kids do this?" she asked, staring at the small cluttered living room.

There was no way she'd be able to study in this environment. Resigned to the fact that she had to do something to make this place look a bit homier, she tossed down her backpack and started attacking boxes. Fortunately, everything she owned didn't take too long to unpack. After arranging dishes in the cabinets, pushing furniture around where she wanted it in her living room and arranging books on her bookshelf, there was no energy left to study. She plugged in her small alarm clock, set it for six in the morning and then collapsed on her bed without even undressing.

Waiting tables for fourteen years made it easy to land a job. The following morning she tied her lacy apron around her waist and eyed the tables that were hers for the morning shift. With little training, she easily fell into the routine at The College Pub, which had hired her on the spot.

"Order up," her boss in the kitchen announced, shoving a long strand of dark hair under his hair net as he smiled at her.

He wasn't bad-looking for a pup. "Thanks, kid," she told him with a wink, balancing the plates of hotcakes and eggs and then working her way to her table.

"Didn't you say you were taking American Lit?" Mary, the other waitress working the morning shift, said when she made her way back to the waitress station.

"Yup. Why?" Thoughts of all that reading hit her. She'd have to save energy after her shift to study until her classes started.

"The guy in the corner. Damn. I'd jump his bones if he'd let me." Mary gestured with her head toward a man hunched over a book in the corner booth. "He's reading an American Lit book. Maybe you could be study partners?"

Mary was a friendly girl and not bad at waiting tables considering she'd never done it before. Typical of her age, she was skin and bones with what had to be an eighteen-inch waist. Men tipped her if she just walked past their tables. Emily vaguely remembered once looking like that. A long, long time ago.

Glancing at the corner booth, the man reading looked up, as if guessing he was being discussed, and lifted his coffee mug to his lips. The first thing that came to mind was that he looked as out of place here as she did. Probably somewhere around her age, brown hair waved naturally around a nicely sculptured face. His eyes were dark, possibly green, with thick eyebrows giving him a mysterious look. For some reason, he didn't strike her as the student type.

Wearing a plain blue T-shirt, his long legs stretched out under the table, she guessed him tall and well built. Broad shoulders made his shirt hug his chest. Sipping slowly at his coffee, his gaze didn't leave hers as he lowered the cup. His mouth moved slightly, not a smile but enough to make her realize she was staring.

"I'd remember him if I'd seen him in class," she said, turning her attention back to her work.

"I'd be getting to know him if I had him in class. But I've always loved older men." Mary let out a sigh then grabbed a clean towel out of the sink full of dish soap.

Handing one to Emily, she moved around the counter, sashaying her hips invitingly as she approached the nearest table to wipe it down.

Emily squeezed excess water from her own white towel and headed toward her tables, eager to get her shift over and get to her homework. The last thing she had time for was romance. Even drooling would distract her. The simple fact was, for the next two years, she'd signed herself to a boring life. It would pay off. She just had to get through it.

No men, she told herself, the thought not helping her mood any.

Stacking plates from the nearest table where several kids had just left, she glanced at the college newspaper, left behind next to her tip. The headline of the thin paper made her freeze.

Woman Murdered in University Parking Lot.

"Oh God," she mumbled, lifting the paper and quickly scanning the article. She turned, carrying her dishes and adding them to the stack of dirty dishes on the cart to haul back to the kitchen.

Still holding the newspaper, she waited until Mary finished with her tables.

"Where is the B parking lot?" she asked, pointing to the article.

"Yeah. I heard about that." Mary shook her head, frowning. "They say some stalker is after older women. You better be careful—no offense."

Emily let the comment slide. "Where's that parking lot?" She tapped her finger on the picture that showed several police cars parked at angles in a large parking lot.

"It's at the bottom of the hill just a couple of blocks from here. Why?"

Emily shook her head, suddenly sick to her stomach. The article said the woman had bled to death. She'd been there. She'd heard her scream. If she hadn't been so damned scared, maybe she could have saved the woman's life.

Shrugging, she tried to sound calm. "Just want to make sure I don't park there."

"It's probably the safest place to park now. They say he never strikes at the same place twice."

"How many murders have there been?" It must have slipped the Admissions Department's mind to inform her they had a serial killer on campus when she'd enrolled.

"There were three last semester, all women, all students who were older, like in their thirties." Mary glanced up at the clock. "This is the first murder this semester. Well, our shift is over."

Concentrating on her reading proved a challenge after seeing that newspaper article. She'd witnessed a murder. She was sure of it. But what good would it do to call the police? The article stated more than she knew. All she'd heard was a cry in the dark. And she'd ignored it.

By the time she needed to head out for her one Thursday night class, her business management class, she could barely remember anything she'd read over the last couple of hours. What a way to start out her college life.

Putting on a clean T-shirt and her last pair of clean jeans, she ran her fingers through her auburn hair, wishing it was a bit longer so she could do something with it. Just a dab of makeup and she was out the door. Reaching campus with ten minutes to spare, there wasn't time to look for a better parking place than the one she'd had the night before.

Dusk settled into night as she climbed the steps and headed toward the Business building. An hour and a half later, she was completely uplifted, believing for the first time that someday owning her own restaurant might be feasible. She liked this professor, her enthusiasm with her lecture contagious.

"Looks like we have a couple of classes together." The jock with all the wrong lines who'd bugged her the night before now stood over her desk as she gathered her things after class.

She looked up at his muscular body, images of the dark shadow racing up the hill the night before coming to mind. Whoever had run away after that woman screamed had been in good shape. Her tummy did a flip-flop. And they liked older women—liked to kill them, that is.

"Looks like it," she said casually, sliding papers into her folder and then slipping it into her backpack.

"What other classes do you have?"

Like she was going to tell him that.

"Enough that I need to get busy studying," she told him, squeezing out of her chair and around him, somehow managing not to touch him.

"You're probably really disciplined." His gaze strolled down her, definitely interested in what he saw.

"More so than you know," she mumbled and turned and walked away.

Realizing the professor put up an announcement of a study group on the chalkboard, she stopped and jotted down the information before heading out the door. Several other students took down the information as well. A lively discussion followed, obviously more than one student sharing her passion for the subject matter. Almost an hour passed before she left the classroom. The hallway was quiet, abandoned, and she hurried along the dark corridor to the glass doors.

Her next class wasn't until Saturday morning, which gave her hope that she could get all the work done for these two classes before seeing what that professor would do to her schedule. Somehow she'd pull this off. Being a student had never appealed to her when she was younger. Living life to its fullest, enjoying casual dating, working enough to pay her bills had been all that mattered for years. Now she wanted more. And she'd get it.

Her backpack tugged at her shoulder, and she adjusted it then tucked a wisp of hair behind her ear as the warm night air made her T-shirt cling to her. It was a farther walk to the parking lot from the business building, and she focused on the sidewalk in front of her, reminding herself again that nighttime was no different than daytime.

Except that it's dark.

Lights caught her eye and she looked up at a small bar across the street from the campus. Several people chatted over beers on the patio. It must be nice to have a social life and manage to go to school as well. Her schedule would turn her into a worse hermit than she was before.

Two people walked to a car parked across the street, making her long for a man. She watched the broad-shouldered guy run his hand up the back of the woman next to him as they walked away from her.

"I've always liked older women." His voice made her slow in her tracks.

It was the same jock who had come on to her twice in the past two days. Here he was using the same line on another woman, and obviously with a bit more luck.

The woman giggled and said something that made his hand move quickly and grab her ass. Yearning flooded through her. Not for that young jock, but for a casual lover. She ached to be touched, fondled, given some attention to help raise her mood so that she could keep on with the crazy schedule she'd dived into. Maybe it wouldn't hurt to get to know a guy or two. Not someone like this young pup, but someone closer to her age, like that guy at work earlier. No-strings sex.

Sheez. And what happened to her orders to avoid romance and keep her thoughts on her studies?

It wouldn't be romance—just sex. She just knew if she looked, there would be a little devil on one of her shoulders and an angel on the other. Shrugging them both away mentally, she watched the couple as the woman moved to unlock her car.

"My place won't work," the jock was saying.

"I guess you can come back to my place for a little bit." The woman turned, the streetlight capturing her smile as she looked up at the jock.

"I bet you can teach me so much." He leaned down to kiss her.

Emily walked past them, neither of them noticing her, and continued on her way. Across the street, folks continued with their idle chatter, the smell of beer and cigarettes drifting toward her.

One man sat alone, not drinking but appearing to be simply staring her way. A second look and she realized it was the man from the diner that morning. Dark shadows hugged his backside, but long muscular legs stretched out under the small wooden table in front of him. He wore jeans and a T-shirt, the same clothes he'd worn that morning. Seeming relaxed, his attention fixed toward her, she found herself heading across the street instead of toward the parking lot.

A car started behind her, the jock finally scoring as he took off with the woman. Halfway across the street, the man from her work stood. Damn. He was tall. And she liked them tall.

Broad shoulders and a muscular chest toned down to flat abs. More than likely he worked out. His dark eyes squinted in her direction and her heart skipped a beat. It had been a while since she'd just walked up to a strange man and introduced herself. In Auburn everyone knew everyone. But this guy might be worth her time. A bit older than most men on campus, he moved like a dangerous predator, confident, all-knowing, with his dark looks adding to that dangerous appeal that melted her insides. A flutter of sexual excitement tightened her tummy.

As she moved closer, the guy reached down and grabbed his backpack, then hurried right past her, not even bothering to look her way.

Emily stopped in her tracks, barely reaching the curb. Her heart sank to a frustrated knot in her gut. That's what she got for thinking she could just pick up some stranger. And what kind of fool was she for thinking that anyway? Like anyone would give her the time of day when there were all these perfect young ladies running around.

Stepping onto the sidewalk, she turned in time to see the guy jump into a new Firebird. He pulled away from the curb quickly, heading the same direction as the couple who'd just left. The bar having lost its appeal, she headed quickly toward the parking lot, forcing thoughts of getting laid out of her head.

Chapter Two

৯৩

Rafe Healy cursed himself for getting distracted. With only five years under his belt as a private investigator, this had been a hell of a job to land. Cracking it would boost his reputation in Kansas City, making him the man for the job.

The junior college didn't want their reputation ruined with a killer on the loose. The police knew about it, obviously, but they weren't moving fast enough to satisfy the school, who didn't want parents yanking their children and enrolling them elsewhere. So they'd pulled Rafe in. His reputation was on the line.

With no leads to go on, and dead bodies showing up every few months, the case had grown frustrating. The chancellor had agreed enrolling in a few classes would bring him closer to the situation. Mingling with kids half his age wasn't easy. But being in the classroom, in the halls, in their environment, gave him an edge the cops didn't have.

Even with that edge, he still didn't have any solid leads. It was only the second day of school and already there had been a murder. Following the stupid jock probably would tell him nothing. He doubted the kid was smart enough to plot and commit murder and not get caught. But he had to eliminate all leads and pray nothing happened while he was off chasing this goon.

When he'd seen that auburn-haired hottie who was in two of the classes he'd enrolled in approaching him, his attention had swerved to her. That had lost him a few minutes.

Rafe hurried to catch up with them, pushing his new Firebird while shifting gears quickly to bring him behind the woman who'd captured herself a young piece of ass.

He wouldn't yell at himself too hard for getting distracted by the lady he was in class with. The woman had tits to die for. And the way they bounced, just a little, was proof enough to know they were real. A man could drown in tits like that. Even though she dressed simply, wearing a T-shirt and faded, comfortable-looking jeans, her slender legs and flat tummy added to the tempting picture she created.

Dark auburn hair waved naturally around her creamy white complexion. He'd seen the light splash of freckles that covered her nose in class. And her expression, relaxed but looking like she would take you on in a second — everything about her had *fuck me please* written all over it.

And that bothered him. This morning while grabbing coffee before heading up to campus, he'd learned she worked at The College Pub. A common stomping ground for college kids, just off campus, the small diner was cheap and the food decent. He'd guessed she was new to the area when she'd asked the other waitress where the parking lot was where the murder happened the night before. Junior College wasn't a large campus. Its parking lots were labeled A through E.

New to the area and fitting the profile perfectly as a candidate for murder didn't sit well with him. Not to mention, it seemed all she took were night classes. She was inviting trouble for herself as long as the killer was loose.

When she'd crossed the street in the dark, it looked as if she gazed directly at him. His dick had hardened instantly. Watching those tits bounce as they came closer had been distraction enough to slow him down. The jock and his lady had taken off before he'd gotten to his car.

Reaching the end of campus, he spotted the small sports car the two had left in and turned the corner, pacing them at about half a block's distance. Tinted windows made it impossible to see what went on inside. The car didn't swerve or change its speed but maintained its course for another mile or so before turning into a large apartment complex predominantly filled with young professionals.

The sign at the entrance of the parking lot said *parking by permit only*. Rafe pulled into guest parking along the outer edge and took his time getting out of the car, watching the couple move toward one of the apartments.

Being a peeping Tom was sometimes part of the job. Although not his most favorite thing to do, if it meant saving a life, he had no problem watching. Pulling out his small pocket camera that was no bigger than a lighter, and actually a damned good buy off eBay, he took a shot of the two walking to the building. Neither of them looked behind them when the quick light flashed and the picture snapped. Sticking the camera in the pocket on his shirt, he strolled across the lot and waited until the two disappeared into a first-floor apartment.

Blinds were pulled over the living room windows, which didn't matter since there was no way he could watch them while visible from the parking lot. Giving them time for some foreplay, he walked around the building, noting which windows from the back would be for that apartment.

As was the case with most complexes, no floodlights protected the backside of the building. Slapping at the mosquito that mistakenly thought it had found supper, he stuck close to the building, listening for any signs that someone else might be outside and nearby.

The seven years he'd spent with KCPD prior to going private offered good experience. He had the advantage now of not sticking out like a cop though. His hair was longer, his clothes plain, and no blatantly obvious unmarked car to hurry to after his job was through. Not to mention, he didn't have to fill out tons of paperwork or justify his actions to anyone. Rafe was after a murderer, and he'd do what it took to capture him.

Bushes lined the backside of the brick building. There were no trees to hide him, but it was a fair distance to the street. Hugging the rough wall, he moved behind the bushes until he reached the window of the apartment the two had entered. Again blinds were closed, but at the right angle, he had a perfect view of the bed. As he guessed, that was where she took her young stud.

Voyeurism wasn't Rafe's thing. Not to mention the young jock was awkward in removing her blouse. The lady smiled coyly when she had to unclasp her bra. And her tits couldn't possibly hold a flame to the auburn-haired woman who'd shot the young jock down twice now. Now that might have been a show worth watching.

A small lamp in the corner of the bedroom offered the only light, casting long shadows off the two lovers as they collapsed on the bed, naked bodies intertwined. The young punk entered her with little foreplay, too anxious to get his dick wet. Lifting her legs to his shoulders, muscles twitched in his back as he began pumping and grinding into her.

Waiting patiently, keeping his reaction to the scene in check, Rafe had little doubt the young punk wouldn't last long. It was what happened afterwards that mattered.

Glancing quickly around him, assuring he wasn't being watched, when he turned his attention back to the small view he had through the side of the blinds, the act was done. It wouldn't surprise him a bit if the act of violence that followed was the woman slapping the jock across the face, pissed at being led on and given no performance. There was no way she could have come in such a short amount of time.

He watched as the two stood, their voices muffled through the wall as they shared idle chitchat. The jock dressed, and the two of them left the room.

Rafe moved along the side of the building, carefully working his way clear of the bushes, keeping an eye to ensure no one spotted him. A door opened and then closed. Stepping into the stairwell, where two doors led to downstairs apartments, and a flight of cement stairs worked its way to the second-floor apartments, Rafe saw the jock sprint across the parking lot.

Deciding to take the long way around the building, he hit the sidewalk approaching the parking lot in time to see the sated jock whistling as he sprinted across the street. Obviously he didn't rate being given a ride home.

Heading toward his car, he allowed his thoughts to drift toward the woman he'd seen approaching him before he'd left the small bar on campus. He could have sworn she was headed toward him, her gaze locked with his. In the dark he couldn't be sure, but it had seemed that way.

The woman was hot. There was no way around it. Her casual walk, her calm confidence and the way she handled the stupid jock who kept trying to pick up on her. Sitting in the back of the classrooms, he'd been able to keep an eye on her. She didn't spend time looking around the room, indifferent to the many looks she got from the guys who tried to get a seat by her.

If this weren't the most important case of his career, he'd go after her. Hell, he'd have her. No matter her cool exterior, there were no doubts he could have her in his bed. A woman like that would probably have to be fucked more than once.

Images of those tits bouncing ever so slightly as she walked toward him once again distracted him momentarily. It took a minute to realize he wasn't imagining it—she actually was in front of him. But she wasn't walking toward him. Instead, she walked across the parking lot, glancing around her as if nervous, and then headed for the apartment the jock had just left.

What the fuck?

He stopped, bending down next to a car as if trying to get in, and watched her through the windows. The odds that she had an apartment right next to the woman who'd just endured bad sex were way too high.

Something wasn't right. Watching, the urge to move in on her, demand to know what she was doing out here, had every muscle in his body tightening. Protector instincts kicked in hard. When she disappeared into the stairwell, he moved closer, taking his time as he weaved around the cars.

Glancing around the parking lot, most stalls were full, and no one was around. His wristwatch said it was almost eleven. What the hell was the damn fool woman doing snooping around the apartments this late at night?

A thought hit him, and it didn't sit well at all. Maybe she was another investigator. He didn't recognize her. Hell, he would have remembered a body like that if he'd seen her before. But why else would she be out here?

He'd moved to the other side of the parking lot and now had a clear view into the stairwell. She was nowhere in sight.

His insides hardened, a predator's instinct surfacing. That woman hadn't just disappeared. Deciding to move in closer, he headed toward the door where the jock had recently left. That's when he noticed it was slightly ajar. A dim light flooded out from the living room, but otherwise, he saw no one.

Rafe almost always wore his shirts untucked. His gun was secured to his belt, hidden by his shirt. He patted the weapon. Running his other hand over the cell phone in his pocket, he moved in closer, curious that the door would be open and no sign of the woman he'd just seen enter the stairwell.

The last row of cars stood between him and the apartment building. He moved between two parked cars when he heard a scream—a bloodcurdling, drawn-out, wailing scream.

"Fuck," he hissed, reaching for his gun.

Someone burst out of the apartment door, a dark figure, halting for a moment when they spotted him and then darting in the opposite direction.

"Wait right there," he yelled, breaking into a full run after them.

Whoever it was was in damned good shape.

By the time he raced to the other end of the stairwell, almost to the point where he'd been minutes before when he'd watched through the window, the person had raced across the field and hit the sidewalk.

Ready to race after them, he stopped in his tracks when he heard another scream, this one lacking the energy of the first, weaker. It was quickly followed by a wail, a cry for help.

Damn it.

Grabbing his cell phone out of his pocket, he hurried toward the apartment door, tempted to leap over a few parked cars. Playing Beaux Duke right now wouldn't make him any more of a hero, not to mention he wasn't as young as he used to be.

"Anyone home?" he asked, nudging the door open with his elbow while holding his gun pointed upward.

A choked cry answered him. Someone appeared at the top of the stairs, just out of his peripheral vision.

"Is everyone okay?" A nervous young man asked from the shadows above him. "Should I call 911?"

Ignoring the young man, he pushed the door open farther then stepped inside the apartment, pointing his gun while quickly taking in his surroundings. Not seeing anyone, he headed toward the bedroom. Then he about gagged.

Quickly dialing 911 himself, he rushed over to the naked woman lying in a pool of blood.

"Send out an ambulance," he quickly told the dispatcher, then gave her the address of the apartment complex.

Staring into the pale blue eyes that looked up at him, he watched the luster fade from them and cursed again. With the amount of stab wounds she'd received, he doubted she'd make it before the ambulance showed. Cringing, he stared at the large dildo stuffed inside her.

The serial killer had struck again.

"Hang in there, baby," he told the woman, kneeling next to her as he pressed fingers to the weak pulse at her neck. "Help is on the way."

Her mouth moved but she didn't speak. Then her eyes fluttered shut, opening again to look at him. Sirens sounded in the distance, and he grabbed the woman's bloodstained hand, squeezing it.

The 911 dispatcher was still on the phone, asking questions.

"Multiple stab wounds. There's blood everywhere. Let me know when they reach the parking lot and I'll go out there to show them which apartment. The numbers are hard to see in the dark." He didn't want to leave the woman, knowing she wouldn't last long.

"I didn't think..." the woman paused, choking on blood as she tried to continue.

The dispatcher told him the ambulance and police had arrived.

"I'll be right back," he told the woman and then rushed out the door.

It was well after midnight when the woman's body was finally carried out of the apartment. The white sheet that covered her from head to toe quickly saturated with blood. Frowning, he walked out of the apartment toward the back of the building, knowing he'd done the right thing but pissed that the killer had slipped out of his fingers.

"It's the same profile as the murder yesterday." Officer Tangari, who'd been on the force when Rafe had, walked up to stand next to him. "Dildo stuffed inside them and multiple stab wounds."

"Watch out what you release to the media. I had the killer right here." Rafe fisted his hands, staring across the dark field the killer had raced across earlier. "You go public on this and they might change their profile."

He'd seen it happen before. The killer got the taste of blood, began craving it. That's where their perpetrator was now. They'd killed one too many times, needed that next murder like a junkie needed a fix. If this hit the papers, became the talk of the town, their perp might slow down or change the profile, make it harder for them to connect the murders.

"We'll get him," Tangari spoke quietly, a trait that had always puzzled Rafe.

The man was large, built like a bulldog, yet had the most soft-spoken tone of voice. It was unnerving at times.

"I saw the killer. He ran off toward the street." Staring across the field, there wasn't a damn thing about the guy he could offer toward a description.

He'd also seen the woman from campus with the big tits. For some reason, he decided to stay quiet about that knowledge for the time being.

The next item on his list though was to learn everything about her. She didn't strike him as a killer. And he knew everyone assumed the murderer was a man. He wouldn't allow any personal attraction to get in his way though. By morning, he would know all there was to know about the woman.

"I'll post more men around campus," Tangari decided.

"Make sure they're discreet. Our guy is getting cocky. We comb the place with uniforms and he'll go dormant, just to pop up again somewhere else where the investigators have nothing on him." Damn it. He wanted to solve this case, not race against the police to solve it.

"We won't be obvious." Tangari looked at him. "The women on campus need protection. I doubt the campus will argue with us upping security. I can put them in plain clothing. But these girls need our protection."

Rafe nodded, turning toward his car. "It's not the younger girls this killer is after."

"I noticed that. So far, all the women have been at least thirty." Tangari followed him through the stairwell into the parking lot.

The ambulance headed out while several police cars still idled in the lot. More than a few tenants stood outside watching, whispering among themselves and watching the police as they moved in and out of the apartment. Several people hovered around one officer, asking more questions than offering information.

"Rafe," Tangari said.

He turned, wishing he knew more about that woman with the big tits. Already she was on his mind again.

"You stay in touch."

Rafe nodded then turned for his car.

* * * * *

Monday morning came too quickly after a weekend of research and staring at a computer screen until his eyes burned. Heading toward The College Pub, he hoped to see the woman who'd distracted too much of his thoughts over the past few days. She was a mystery, and one he planned to solve. The other morning when he'd been here, she'd come in after him, around seven-thirty. This morning he strolled down the block, having parked conveniently in front of The College Pub and then pretending to browse in front of a few shop windows. Glancing down the street, his insides tightened. Damn he loved watching those big tits bounce as she hurried down the street toward him.

Walking with her head down and her apron flapping in her hand at her side, Rafe took his time putting her image to memory. As if it wasn't already there.

Her auburn hair was still damp and darker, almost dark brown. It fell to her shoulders, straight, without bangs, a natural look that he'd always enjoyed on a woman. She wore tight blue jeans and a snug T-shirt tucked in, showing off a flat tummy and slender thighs. Her legs were thin and she wore comfortable tennis shoes.

With her gaze focused down as she approached, Rafe took in her long lashes, her slender nose that tilted just slightly at the end. Her creamy skin didn't appear to have a blemish on it.

She wasn't petite, but small-boned, hardly the body of a murderess.

And exactly what kind of body does a murderer have?

When she reached the entrance of The College Pub, she looked up, seeing him for the first time. Certainly a murderess would be more attentive to who was around her.

Then she froze, staring at him as her lips parted. Full lips with a dark glossy lipstick making them shimmer, they slowly formed an enticing circle. Her eyes were light blue, accented with enough makeup to make them look larger than they probably were.

As she stared at him, those eyes of hers darkened, suddenly looking like a thunderhead ready to explode.

"Are you following me?" she asked, her voice a deadly whisper.

"Maybe." He watched her lips form a thin line, disgust apparent in her expression.

"Well, stop it." And with that, she turned and entered The College Pub, her ass swaying nicely before she disappeared from sight.

Chapter Three

ဢ

"Will you help me with this?" Emily stood toward the back of the kitchen, turning her back as she held on to her apron strings.

"Sure." Mary popped her gum as she grabbed the strings, tying the apron securely to Emily's waist. "Why are you shaking like a leaf?"

"You know those murders that happened this past week?" she asked, turning to look at Mary and then over Mary's shoulder at Carlos who flipped pancakes over the large flat grill.

"There was only one murder," Carlos said in his thick Mexican accent.

"There were two," Emily corrected him. "And I witnessed the second one." She'd witnessed the first one too. She just hadn't realized it at the time.

"What?" both Carlos and Mary said at the same time.

Pushing thoughts of how she might have helped the woman attacked the first time, she focused on the two of them as they gawked at her.

"I thought maybe I knew who it was. And I followed him. But I was wrong. And now everything is really confusing." She lowered her voice, looking past them toward the tables out in the diner.

Both Carlos and Mary turned and looked that direction too, then looked back at her.

"You're crazy," Mary said, putting her hands on her hips. "I mean like, you're old enough to be one of the women killed."

Emily exhaled. "And that's why I've got to look out for myself. I didn't tell anyone, but I was in that parking lot last week when that first woman was killed. I heard her scream."

For a moment none of them said anything. Carlos had been staring at her and quickly turned to give the cooking food his attention.

"You should tell the police this," he said, shaking his thick mop of black hair barely contained in his hairnet.

"I don't really have anything to tell them." She thought about the man standing outside when she'd walked to work.

His penetrating gaze had speared through her. With one glance, moisture soaked her panties. It sucked how such a dominating gaze, his aggressive stance, made her body throb with need.

She'd seen him Friday night after she'd arrived at the complex where that stupid jock had gone with that poor woman. The jock had his fun, left, and then the poor woman had been killed. For all Emily knew, the jock probably didn't even know it happened. And the good-looking guy who'd been there, and then outside just now. What was his story? She'd asked if he'd been following her and he'd said, *maybe*.

Maybe.

"She doesn't have anything to tell the cops," Carlos said, sounding disgusted. "Your orders are up, Mary. Emily, are you going to work today?"

"Yes." She hurried past them, grabbing her order pad and taking a look out in the diner.

She froze when the man she'd threatened at the door now sat in one of the booths, in her section. Mary almost ran into her, halting just before a tray of food hit the floor.

"Damn," Mary swore under her breath.

"Sorry," Emily mumbled.

Chewing her lip, she turned back to Carlos. "You've run this place for a couple years now, right?"

When Carlos had interviewed her, she'd envied how young he was and that he owned his own place. He had the same degree she worked toward now. After graduating, he found funding that had something to do with him being a minority. His parents weren't in the States, and he helped support them as well as a younger brother who came in after school to wash dishes. Emily hadn't met him.

"Yeah. Why?" He ran a long blade over the grill, pushing pieces of pancakes into the tray at the edge as he readied it for the next meals he would prepare.

Staring at the deadly-looking blade, so commonly used to scrape grease and food from the flat metal grill, thoughts of the women's screams rushed through her. Icy chills rushed down her back. Sucking in a breath, she pointed toward the dining area.

"That man out there, in the booth by the window. Does he come in here often?"

Carlos glanced past her, leaning his stocky body slightly so that he could see. Wiping his thick hands on his long white apron, he shook his head.

"Never seen him before." He met her gaze and winked. "You want me to get his number for you?"

"No." She frowned and then turned, leaving the kitchen.

The knowledge that he was in the diner sparked her nerve endings, igniting a fire inside her too hard to ignore. She didn't have to look at him. Even with her back turned, his image burned into her mind's eye. Reacting to a stranger like this was stupid.

Regardless of his intense sex appeal, it bothered her that he'd been at the murder scene the other night. She'd bolted the hell out of there when the woman started screaming, again fleeing instead of investigating. But terror had ripped through her.

Why had he been there? When he'd been at the bar on campus at the same time that the jock had been there. Then later at the complex. Coincidence? No way.

Thinking that he could be guilty of some heinous crime sent shivers through her. While she'd been there, he hadn't gone into one of the apartments, given no indication that he lived there. He'd loitered in the parking lot, hugging shadows. Not the way a normal person acted.

If it threatened her job, she'd explain later, but there was no way she'd wait on that man.

What if he's the murderer?

Thirty minutes later the man obviously got the hint that he wasn't going to get service from her. She heaved a sigh when finally he got up and left the place. It was a damned shame really—the man was hotter than hell. But seeing him last Friday night, right after that murder, when she knew he'd been at the bar on campus before the couple left, just didn't sit right with her.

Being scared of the dark didn't help when murder was on your mind.

Emily rushed across campus, hurrying to get to her restaurant management class, knowing at least for that hour she'd have no confrontation with anyone suspicious. As always, the class flew by, and then with trepidation she crossed the street to the building where her English class was.

Over the weekend she'd rehearsed in her mind how she'd determine if the young jock knew about the murder of the woman he'd fucked the other night. Oddly enough though, he wasn't in class.

There weren't many seats left when she hurried into the classroom, Professor Jenkins already scratching chalk across the chalkboard. Sitting toward the back of the room, adjusting books on his desk, sat the man she'd encountered that morning at The College Pub. There were several free desks, all of them surrounding him.

Damn.

Her heart raced as she walked down the narrow aisle, avoiding feet and backpacks, and took the seat next to him.

"Not ignoring me today?" He had beautiful green eyes that at the moment almost appeared amused.

God. They were bedroom eyes, the kind that could make her come just staring into them.

"Behave and I won't," she whispered, her hands shaking as she dropped her backpack on the desk and purposely kept her eyes on the professor.

Having managed to read everything required for tonight's class, Emily enjoyed the lecture, aching to raise her hand more than once and comment on Professor Jenkins' lectures. When finally a discussion began, she found herself chiming in, her thoughts relaxing and enjoying the discussion of American literature.

The class groaned when Professor Jenkins reminded them of the next one hundred pages due at the following lecture. The lighthearted atmosphere from the current discussion didn't sway though.

"Let's head down to the bar and get a beer," the girl in front of her suggested to several others when the class began moving, gathering backpacks and heading for the door.

More than anything Emily would love to join them. Just imagine, stimulating conversation in a bar. Never would she have guessed her life would have taken a turn like this, that she'd be in an environment where people, young people, wanted to go get a beer and talk about Anais Nin.

"Don't forget the outline for your research paper must be approved by next Monday." Professor Jenkins barely got his words out over the chatter in the classroom.

Well hell.

Having absolutely no idea what she would do her paper on, Emily decided maybe a quick trip to the library while she was still on campus would be a smarter move than enjoying a few brews with a bunch of kids and talking about something other than being laid off, or cheating husbands.

Sitting next to the good-looking stranger managed to be more of a distraction than she cared to admit. When she left the classroom, he was on her heels, not saying anything but right there. A shadow, stuck to her, moving as she did—she swore if she turned around he'd still remain behind her, just out of view of her peripheral vision. Like a ghost, there but not quite visible.

Deciding to ignore him, she made it out of the building and halfway across the lawn before his presence made her nuts.

Turning quickly, it shouldn't have surprised her that he anticipated her movement and stopped before walking into her.

"Why are you following me?" she demanded, more than aware of the fact that the people around them were moving away quickly, leaving her alone in the darkness on campus.

"And what makes you think I am?" he asked, those green eyes glowing in the darkness.

"Then where are you headed?" she challenged him.

He shrugged, such a slight movement of one shoulder that she almost missed it. "To my car," he said.

Staring at him possibly a moment longer than she should have, his closed lips forming a straight line and strong cheek bones giving his expression a dominating tone, she decided this wasn't a man easily countered.

Turning around just as abruptly, she continued her pace, fighting not to hurry, although not dawdling either, she reached the long stone steps to the library. Climbing them, the man behind her, still being her shadow, reached over her and held the door as she entered.

Again she turned quickly, glaring. "Your car is parked inside the library?"

God. She swore amusement made his face even sexier. One side of his mouth curved up slightly as he looked down at her.

"No," he said without hesitating, stopping so that he was inches from her. "I decided to follow you."

He admitted it. Before her jaw could fall in surprise, she turned, her hair flying over her shoulder, and hurried inside the library. Never having been there before, it took her a minute to get her bearings. Rows of computers, with students at each one of them, were to her left. Shelved books seemed to carry on for miles beyond that. Ahead of her was a large sign, giving directions on how to get around in the library. She walked up to it, although for the life of her, with him still right behind her, there was no way she could focus on the different subjects listed and what part of the library was what. Some kind of color-coded chart was explained but she couldn't focus on the words.

"You're Emily Rothmeier." His voice was barely a whisper.

Shit. He knew her name. She fought to keep her composure when a warm flush spread through her as way too many reasons why he might have gone to the effort of learning her name rushed through her frazzled brain.

"And you are?" she asked without thinking.

Damn it. Like she wanted him to think she cared at all what his name was.

Hell yes, she wanted him to think that. More than that. The ache to know him, know his touch, robbed her of her sensibility. If only he'd reveal any indication that he wanted her too.

God. She had lost her fucking mind. A stranger. He was a complete stranger.

"Rafe Healy." His hand moved, and she took a step backward.

He had a way of moving his lips so that a half smile appeared. It made him look cocky. Damn his sex appeal anyway. She willfully turned her attention back to the chart in front of her, this time focusing on the map of the place. Finding the thing too damned confusing, the only thing she could do was find a librarian. She couldn't remember the last time she'd been in a library.

"I'm a private investigator." He'd pulled a wallet out of his back pocket and flipped it open, holding a card out for her to see.

His words brought all thoughts of learning how to use the library out of her head. Staring at him, and then the wallet he held out for her to examine, his words sunk in slowly.

A private investigator. Now her mouth did hang open. Licking her suddenly too dry lips, she took his wallet from him, the soft worn leather warm in her hand. Her hand trembled slightly, and her fingers were damp, sticking to the wallet as she studied the card behind the plastic casing.

Rafe D. Healy. Age thirty-two. Licensed as a private investigator in the state of Missouri. She studied the picture of the man in the corner of the card and then without permission flipped the card and found his driver's license. Not as good of a picture, but then no one ever took good pictures for their license.

Rafe reached for his wallet, his fingers closing over hers, warm and strong, holding her hand and his wallet in a firm grip.

"Well, that explains..." she began, staring at their hands, her small whiter hand held in his larger hand.

"It doesn't explain everything," he said quietly.

She looked up at that intent expression on his face. Looking at him in this new light, knowing he was an investigator, probably assigned to find the murderer, allowed her to enjoy his sex appeal even more.

Suddenly it was too damned warm in that library. She'd enjoyed a few lovers in the past but in the past month, since she'd moved here, there hadn't been time to think about sex. Or when she had, she'd pushed it out of her mind as something that wasn't an option.

But now...

"What doesn't it explain?" She let her gaze drop to his broad shoulders.

"I want to know what you were doing at that apartment complex the other night." His voice remained soft, almost a rumbling whisper.

Shifting gears from undressing him took a moment. She looked up at his face. His question sank through her like molasses, slow and heavy. His expression wasn't readable. No worry lines around his eyes or mouth, nothing to indicate why he'd want to know why she'd been there. If he were a detective, he'd question those he thought might be guilty. Suddenly her heart caught in her throat.

"I haven't done anything wrong," she told him, then turned from him, heading toward the information counter.

Rafe left her alone as she learned where the books were that she needed to start her research. She was all thumbs pulling paperwork out of her backpack and stuttered more than once discussing where possible books might be for her project.

Gritting her teeth, she ordered her heart to quit pounding as she headed toward the elevator that would take her to the lower levels of the library.

Rafe slipped into the elevator with her just as the doors slid closed.

"Running from me implies guilt." He crossed his arms over his chest and corded muscles stretched.

"Running from you?" She cocked an eyebrow then forced herself not to look at him. "I thought I'd answered your question already."

"Hardly."

The elevator doors slid open and Emily stepped out quickly, glancing at the piece of paper where'd she'd jotted down numbers and then at the rows of books that seemed to go on forever, fading into darkness. It wasn't as well lit down here, with cement floors that added to the feeling of suddenly being in a forgotten basement. Anything could happen down here.

Ignoring his comment, she made a show of trying to figure out what row of books she needed. Focusing on anything other than him behind her was nearly impossible. Her palms were sweaty, her insides jittery, and the silence of the basement stacks sent an eerie sensation through her. As much as Rafe unnerved her, moving silently behind her, other than the quiet thud of his footsteps, she was almost grateful not to be down here alone.

"You witnessed that murder," he whispered from behind her.

She'd stepped into a long aisle, rows of books with their musty smell climbing both sides of her. That dark intent expression of his was hard to read.

Nodding, she glanced down at the paper in her hand. He'd said murder, and not murders. He didn't know she'd been there for the first one too.

"Why were you there, Emily?" His tone was soothing, caressing her. Whispering, yet making his question somehow a demand, had her opening her mouth to answer.

Letting out a sigh, she stared at him for a moment.

"Because I wanted to know if that stupid punk was the murderer," she confessed.

Something twitched in his jaw, a small muscle, barely noticeable except that she'd already been staring at him.

"You were out late at night trying to chase down a potential crime?" The disbelief in his tone wasn't missed.

Just because she had never been anything other than a waitress didn't make her stupid. Scowling, she turned her attention to the books, noting the numbers on them and fighting to concentrate so she could find the section she needed.

"It was a crime, and I saw the murderer." A shiver rushed through her as she remembered barely having time to cower behind the building when someone had rushed out of the apartment.

It had all happened so quickly. The jock had left, but then someone had come from around the building, barely giving her time to cower in the shadows before they'd entered the apartment. Her gut had told her to creep toward the partially opened door, but when she'd heard the screams, she'd frozen. Someone had bolted out of the apartment, running past her into the field so quickly she hadn't noticed much about them. Then Rafe had appeared, yelling and ready to race after them, until the woman inside the apartment had screamed again.

"Tell me what you saw." He obviously realized how the memory shook her up because he rested a firm hand on her shoulder.

The heat from his touch sent all thoughts of the ugly crime into a misty whirlwind in her mind. Strong fingers pressed against her flesh through her shirt, making her insides quicken.

"The murderer moved too quickly." She exhaled, wishing for better control of her senses.

Rafe churned her insides into a craving puddle of smoldering need.

"Do you realize how much danger you put yourself in?" he asked, a dangerous whisper that chilled her skin.

"I can take care of myself." She had been for years.

Rafe turned her, forcing her to face him, and his other hand came up so that he pinned her arms. Unable to move, and not sure that she would be able to even if he didn't hold her in place, she focused on that muscular chest.

A stranger had grabbed her in an isolated area of the basement library. He spoke of danger, yet the position he put her in was just as potentially dangerous. Her heart thudded against her ribs as heat rushed through her. Frustration mixed with desire. No man ever manhandled her. She wouldn't have it. But at the same time, the way he grabbed her, forced her to face him and stared down at her with such a predatory gaze made her heartbeat fall to between her legs.

One hand brushed over her shoulder and then gripped her chin, forcing her to look up at him. Those thick eyebrows shaded his intense green eyes. God, he was gorgeous.

Cupping her chin, holding her head just the way he wanted it, he pressed his lips to hers. Fire scoured her senses. Demanding and aggressive, he parted her lips with the flick of his tongue and then impaled her mouth.

A groan escaped him and his hands moved quickly, pulling her against him. Talk about a rock-hard body. Her breasts pressed against his chest, which felt like solid steel. It took every inch of her self-control to keep her hands from wandering down him so that she could test out the length of his cock, feel how hard he was.

His lips moved over hers, taking all she offered and making it clear he wanted more. Opening her, forcing her head back, his tongue probed, rough and then softer, deepening his exploration.

Running her tongue around his, she wasn't too shy to explore herself. He tasted of coffee and smelled of something more masculine, more carnal, that had her insides spinning. No longer did she care that they were in a public library, alone in the stacks buried deep underground. It didn't matter that anyone could walk up on them, that she barely knew him. With that kiss, he unleashed such powerful need she wanted to beg him to fuck her right there.

His hands barely moved. A finger caressed her shoulder, the slightest of movements that about undid her. And the way he cupped her chin, forceful, determined, preventing her from moving her face unless she put up a fight.

And at the moment, she had no fight in her.

His mouth left hers and for a moment she couldn't open her eyes, her mouth still parted, her lips swollen and wet while she focused on remembering how to breathe. She still felt his hand on her shoulder when he let go of her and then ran his hand down her front, brushing over her sensitive nipple.

"I don't want to see you playing detective again," he said.

When she opened her eyes, he was a blur in front of her. Her breasts had swelled with need, her nipples aching for his mouth. The throbbing between her legs distracted her thoughts. It took a moment for his words to register.

"I wasn't playing anything," she said, her voice a scratchy whisper. She cleared her throat, taking a step backward when she ached to walk back into his arms. "Someone out there is killing women my age. I'd rather catch them before they catch me."

His expression hardened, that twitch returning at the side of his mouth. "And you're an expert on the thinking of an insane killer?"

"What makes you think they're insane?" She ran her hand over the backs of the books in front of her, their different colors and sizes running together as she stared at them. "Seems someone who can pull off murder after murder and not get caught would have to be pretty damned sane and alert to what is going on around them."

"So you're the expert?" Now he mocked her.

And she realized at that moment that he'd kissed her to gain her confidence. Albeit his intention was probably to protect her, it was still the act of a player of sorts. He played her to gain her trust. The thought made her heart weigh heavy in her chest. She should accept the fact, possibly get to the point with him where she could enjoy some good sex. If how he kissed was any indication, he'd probably make one hell of a lover.

"No. I'm no expert," she admitted quietly. "And you're right. What I did was dangerous."

"Yup." He was watching her.

She knew without looking. Somehow he worked to determine something about her, and she wasn't sure what it was. At the same time, it didn't make sense that her heart weighed so heavily just because she believed his kiss meant something different than she wanted it to mean.

"Well, it's late. And I have to get up early." She crossed her arms over her chest, a shield over her heart, which did little good.

"What about your books?" He gestured to the shelves on either side of them.

"I know where to look now. I'll come back tomorrow."

"Then I'll walk you to your car."

She shook her head, moving around him. He stepped to the side, allowing her room. Somehow walking past him was harder to do than she imagined. He was like some fucking sex magnet, pulling her toward him while she fought to keep her distance.

"You should be out looking for the killer. Thanks for the warning." Suddenly her eyes burned and that pissed her off.

No way would she let herself get all mushy over some guy. No matter that he had more sex appeal than most men did in their little finger. She wouldn't think about the fact that he was a better kisser than any man she'd ever kissed before.

Her muscles twitched in her legs, and somehow she managed to get around him without stumbling into him. Heading back toward the elevator, the urge to run, get away from him, made her quicken her pace. She had to keep moving or she'd turn around and fling herself into his arms. Anger rushed through her. No way would he play her like this.

She reached the elevator and stabbed at the white button on the wall next to it. It opened without making her wait.

"No." She held out her hand, stopping Rafe when he would have entered the elevator with her. "I want to ride up alone. Good luck with your investigation."

He stared at her for only a moment. The door began closing and he put his foot forward, stopping it.

"Like hell," he said, storming his way into the elevator with her. "I'm walking you to your car."

There was nothing she could do to make him get out of the small compartment.

"Look. I understand that you felt a need to gain my confidence," she began, looking down at his thick thighs, at the way hard muscles pressed against his snug-fitting jeans. "I'm sure many detectives use whatever method works best to protect women who get in the way of their investigations. But I'm not some young college girl."

"So that's how it is." His tone turned hard, cold. "I kissed you so that you'd do what I say."

She didn't say anything. Nervous sweat dampened her skin under her shirt. Suddenly he sounded angry, like she'd offended him.

"What would I be accomplishing if I kissed you again?" He took a step toward her. "What would I be accomplishing if I followed you home and fucked you?"

There was nowhere to back up to escape the way he stepped into her personal space.

He gripped her chin, forcing her to look up at him—just the way he had when he'd kissed her minutes before. His voice lowered to a whisper. "And what would I be accomplishing if I made you scream my name when your orgasm ripped through you?"

The elevator door opened but there was no way she could move. Staring into those hard green eyes, witnessing a rippling of emotions surge through him as she watched, something else occurred to her. Rafe Healy had a temper, and she'd just pissed him off.

Swallowing hard, she almost ripped her face from his grip, marching around him and out into the quiet library. Heading toward the exit, his questions rang in her head. Why would he ask her such things? What kind of man was he?

Tingles brushed over her skin. Damn it if his daring nature wasn't one hell of a turn-on.

She'd made it down the stairs of the library, the warm night air making nervous sweat cling to her body, when he fell into stride next to her. Glancing his way, she saw how hard his expression was, how set his jaw was.

"So which one are you going to do?" she asked him, deciding he would see that she could be daring too.

Besides, something inside her ached to know him better.

"What?" he asked, blinking as he gave her his attention. It was as if she'd pulled him out of some far-off thought.

That confused her. Frowning, she decided to push the issue.

"Are you going to kiss me? Fuck me? Or make me scream your name during an orgasm?"

The stormy expression lifted and that half smile he did so well appeared on his face. "More than likely all three."

She almost stumbled over the curb when they reached the street. That would be good. Let him say something so fucking suggestive and then she makes an ass out of herself, falling on her face. She regained her footing quickly. And her composure. Working as a waitress for years made her stronger than this. No man would get the better of her.

Racing to think of a good comeback, something caught her eye when they crossed the street. The stairs ahead of them faded into dark shadows. The cement parking lot spread out like a black sea below them. Sparsely lit with streetlamps that splattered light over areas of the lot and then faded into darkness, parts of the lot glowed against the blackness.

The stairs were wide enough for them to descend next to each other. Her car came into view, shrouded with bright light. She'd conveniently parked in a spot where the light was the brightest. But as she stared, there seemed to be movement around her car, a shadow appearing and then disappearing, trying not to be seen.

"Maybe you should pay to get a permit to park up here on the street," Rafe said when they reached the stairs. "Which car is yours?"

She wasn't about to get into a discussion about her budget with him. No matter that she'd been talking to him for less than an hour, it wasn't that hard to figure out he was the controlling type. She pointed through the darkness.

"The tan Buick," she said, distracted as she tried to get her eyes to focus on the image that she wasn't even sure was there.

In the deep shadows, a chill almost rushed over Emily even though the evening air was warm. Fall was around the corner, but the lazy days of summer still persisted. Her car was parked as she'd left it earlier that night, and a quick scan didn't show anything out of the ordinary. Maybe her senses were simply on red alert, her body one huge nerve ending, and that had enabled her to see things that weren't there. Shadows could play a trick on the eye too.

Letting out a quiet sigh of relief, she adjusted her backpack to pull out her keys. Still holding the paper with the numbers on it from the library, she awkwardly unzipped her pouch, stuffed the paper in there then fumbled for her keys.

"Thanks for walking me to my car," she said, not looking up.

"Emily." The way he said her name, a rough grumble, need rushing through the one word, had her looking up quickly.

This time he didn't grip her chin. Rafe leaned into her, brushing his lips over hers.

"I didn't kiss you simply to get you to comply," he told her.

Just a mere brush of lips, hardly any contact at all, sent her heart into an erratic beat that she couldn't control.

"Then why did you?" she asked, barely able to speak through her quick breaths.

"Because you're sexy as hell and I couldn't help myself."

"Damn good answer." She couldn't help but smile at him.

Those deep green eyes of his twinkled, obviously pleased that he'd made points. Unlocking her door, she tossed her backpack into the car and then slid behind the steering wheel, torn between offering him a ride to his car or simply saying goodnight.

"Tomorrow morning, serve me breakfast." He winked at her, tapped her nose with his finger and then turned and left, those snug jeans hugging damn sexy legs as he walked away from her to the stairs.

Chapter Four

ॐ

He waited until the guy who'd kissed her walked away. Controlling his anger, his jealousy, which came in such strong waves that his muscles bulged, hurting under his flesh, he held his squatting position. Ignoring the cramping in his muscles, refusing to move while pain distorted his senses, he watched. The man ascended the stairs, finally leaving them alone.

It wasn't right that she'd turned him down—twice. Yet here she was, listening to the bullshit from that man about kissing her and then letting him kiss her again.

"Emily," he said, proud of how he kept his tone calm, showing none of his anger.

Mom would be proud.

She hadn't shut her door yet. Her hand was on the handle. The way she turned, let out a cry, her delicate hand flying into the air, as if trying to protect herself, made him smile. There weren't many things that made him smile these days.

"I didn't mean to scare you." He gripped the top of her car door, preventing her from closing it.

Her blue eyes were large, mascara outlining them nicely. His gaze only remained on her terrified expression for a moment. That T-shirt of hers hugged those large tits. He could rip that material from her. Watching her breasts spring free of their confinement would be an incredible sight.

"Well, you did. What are you doing sneaking around my car?" She started her engine, her gaze moving to his hand on her door.

"I missed class and wanted to know if I could get the assignment. When I saw you with the old guy there, I didn't want to ruin your moment. Like I said, I'm sorry I scared you."

"That old guy, as you call him, is my age," she said defensively. "Why did you skip class?"

Thoughts of his wife yelling at him, calling him stupid, brought down his mood. He fought to hold on to the adrenaline that had filled him while hiding and waiting, counting the seconds until he could be alone with Emily.

"It was a family matter." He shrugged.

Emily bit her lip, barely nodding. Her gaze traveled around the isolated parking lot. No one was anywhere near them. Fear made her face grow pale. Pussies often got wet when a woman was scared. Mom had told him so.

He'd tried to make his wife scared, but it never worked. She was just like Mom. Funny that the two of them hated each other. No matter what he did, his wife's pussy never got wet. Dry and rough. He hated putting his cock in her.

But Emily, she was sincerely scared. His dick got hard just thinking about how her pussy would feel around his cock.

"The assignment is in your syllabus. You don't need me to give it to you." She shifted and accelerated so quickly that the car door ripped out of his hand.

Turning her car quickly, she closed her door and sped away from him.

Beaux Robinson stood in the parking lot, the light from the street lamp glowing down on him. He imagined its warmth, turning to stare up at it until it burned his retina, leaving a black orb imprinted on his vision.

Mom would like Emily Rothmeier. His wife would hate her. He didn't understand women. So much alike, yet so different.

Returning home to his wife, listening to her call him names and cut him down, didn't sound appealing at the moment. But going to Mom wouldn't work either. Her needs were growing daily it seemed. He did everything he could to make her happy, make her content. Between Mom and his wife, he barely had time to make himself happy.

And that's what he needed to do right now. Breaking into a jog, feeling the adrenaline rush through him, he headed toward the stairs, bounding up them while listening to his heart pound in his chest. He was barely winded when he reached the top.

It had been a shame he hadn't been able to make it to class. By now he'd have some nice hot cunt to sink his dick into if he'd managed to get up on to campus earlier. It was all his wife's fault. God, he hated her.

Mom had said she'd be a good wife to have though.

"A good woman always walks alongside a good man. Darlene will offer no interference." Remembering how Mom whispered the words always had a soothing effect. "She knows better."

And Mother was always right. After a year of marriage, he still hadn't figured out what Mom had meant. All his wife did was yell at him. She wouldn't put out but then was furious when he went out and fucked other women. Mom approved though. Mom had even told his wife that. He'd leave that for the two of them to battle out. Right now campus was too quiet, and he needed to get laid.

Heading toward the bar, his cell phone rang and he pulled it out of his pocket, noting the number before answering.

"What do you want?" he asked after answering.

"Where are you?" His wife had adopted a hard tone to her voice that she hadn't had when he'd met her.

He sighed. "Where I always am."

"On campus? At this hour?"

"When will you understand?" She was bringing him down.

Her incessant whining and nagging was only the beginning. Tonight already showed signs of being unproductive. And the only thing worse than his pain in the ass wife was the disappointed look his mother would give him when he couldn't help her tonight.

"Understand what? That you don't love me?" There it went. Her tone hitting that pitch that started the ringing in his head.

"You know what Mom said." It was hard to hear his voice over the ringing. He put his palm to his forehead but it didn't do any good.

There was silence for a moment. Even his wife understood the reverence of Mom. He relished the moments without her voice coming through the small phone. Looking ahead of him at the lights coming from the bar, he didn't notice anyone outside. He'd have to go in, see who was there. Mom told him how he was blessed to be so good-looking. Life was easy when you were good-looking. You got what you wanted if you had good looks. But right now it wasn't a want, it was a need.

He had to fuck.

"You never had this obsession with your mother before we got married. I don't know what's wrong with you. What's wrong with me?"

"I'll tell you what's wrong with you," he sneered. "Your pussy is so dry it hurts my cock. A good wife should fuck her husband. This is all your fault."

"You fucking bastard," she yelled. "You're fucking every woman in town. You're a slut. God only knows what I might catch if I let you inside me."

No. He wasn't fucking every woman in town. His wife didn't understand. The ringing started again, burning through his head so that he could hardly walk.

"Don't call me names." He could barely speak. "You know what happens when you call me names."

"Yeah, yeah. The voices. God. I swear you're insane." She hung up on him.

She always hung up on him. Beaux didn't understand why she even bothered to call him sometimes. All she did was yell and then hang up.

Stuffing his cell phone in his pocket, his hand brushed against his groin next to his relaxed cock. Time to find some action.

The voices hadn't come, the echoed screams of ghosts best forgotten. As he strolled across the street, the ringing in his head slowly subsided. Inhaling deeply as he walked into the small bar, Beaux was instantly disappointed that only three people were inside, playing darts in the corner. All young skinny runts. No women.

The bored bartender held a bar rag in his hand, looking at him expectantly. Beaux frowned. Turning around, he left the place.

Mom would be disappointed. He hated that. She made him feel so guilty. And it wasn't his fault. None of it was his fault.

He knew the rules. Mom's needs were growing, but she insisted on the rules. But hell, he had needs too. Heading toward his car, he decided it wouldn't kill him to look for some willing bitch off campus. Just this once. Maybe Mom didn't have to know about it.

Mom knew everything. Even if he didn't tell her, she always knew everything.

He'd barely reached his car when the ringing started again. Thinking about some of the bars downtown, places where college kids hung out, faded as the ringing grew. He hurried to get in his car, struggling to dig his keys out of his pocket. The ringing increased, making his brain burn.

Stretching his legs, his feet pressed against the floor of the car while his back pushed against the back of the seat, he clung to the steering wheel. His teeth clamped together, but he wouldn't close his eyes.

"Please no voices," he whispered through his teeth, hardly hearing his own words.

The ringing was like a drill, high-pitched and piercing through his skull. Tearing through his brain, intensifying, there was no way he could focus on anything around him anymore. But still, he wouldn't close his eyes.

Close your eyes and you won't see anything.

It was a lie.

Hum. Hum to yourself and you won't hear anything.

Another lie.

The moaning. It always started with the moaning.

"No. Mom. No." Beaux shook his head.

Too late. They were here. The voices had arrived. The only blessing they offered was that the ringing stopped. But he'd endure the pain. He'd relish the pain. Anything not to hear the voices.

What are you doing? God. No! What are you going to do?

Damn slut. You lie in my bed naked and ask what am I doing?

Once the voices started, the pain when they paused was unbearable. Beaux stared wide-eyed, not seeing the darkness outside his car or the isolated street. There weren't buildings surrounding him anymore or the nicely landscaped lawns of campus. Not for Beaux. The voices had invaded, consuming him.

He waited, listening carefully. The silence was awful, especially when he knew what happened next.

Plunge! It was a soft spongy sound. Beaux jumped even though he'd been waiting for it. *Plunge! Plunge!* He swore he could hear the knife slice through the air, cutting wickedly before it made contact. *Plunge!*

You're nothing! Fucking trash!

God! No! Stop! And that's when the screams started. He never understood why they took so long, but they always did. Maybe it was shock. Not many people got to witness so much blood, flowing rich and dark. It was amazing how it splashed, red dots splattering everywhere.

Is this what you want? Is this what you live for? At your age, you should love something like this!

Please. Don't.

But you love this. I saw you. You begged for it.

Not like this. No.

Yes. Take all of it. Beg for more!

Plunge!

Beaux realized he'd stopped breathing and gasped for air. It took a minute for him to realize why the air smelled so fresh. There was no rich metallic smell. Looking around him, confused for a moment, he remembered that he sat in his car. He was alone.

The voices were gone.

Shaking, he managed to let go of the steering wheel, his hands hurting. It was hard to swallow, and he was too big to move easily in the confines of his car. After a minute, he managed to pull his phone out of his pocket.

He couldn't think. Every time it was as if his brain was wiped clean, swiped with a thick white cloth, erasing the red dots on the wall, the cloth also erased his brain. He stared into the darkness at his small phone, at the buttons on it. Then slowly, he punched in the numbers and pushed send.

"Mom?" his voice cracked. "Mom? The voices came back."

"It's okay, baby. Mom will take care of everything. Come here, sweetheart."

Mom always knew what to say.

Beaux smiled, relaxing. He started the car, his breathing slowly returning to normal.

"I'm coming, Mom. I'm coming."

Chapter Five

ॐ

Rafe stretched his legs, hating the wooden chairs facing Joe Simpson desk. The same chairs had faced Simpson's desk since Rafe was a rookie with the KCPD. They were uncomfortable, made a person stiff within minutes, and Simpson knew it. He liked keeping anyone he interrogated at a disadvantage.

Simpson, head of the Homicide Department, leaned back in his chair, his elbows on the arm rests while he pressed his hands together and tapped his lips. Rafe knew the man was doing anything but praying. He watched him intently.

"Just because you don't work for the department anymore doesn't mean I'm going to give you free rein with this investigation." Simpson didn't move his hands when he spoke.

Rafe didn't bother to tell the older man that he had no control over what Rafe did. Simpson had his respect, but he wasn't part of the force anymore. He answered only to himself, the way he worked best.

Dean Wood stood with his back to all of them, staring out the narrow window at the view of downtown Kansas City. "I won't have a competition playing out between you all," he said. The man had a commanding voice, sounding more like a drill sergeant than a man of education. "This isn't a contest. We have someone killing women on my campus and I want it stopped."

"That's why I called this meeting." Simpson looked over at Tangari, who sat next to Rafe. "We know you've hired Healy here to work on this case and the best way to handle matters is if we all work together."

Rafe knew why he'd been asked to come down to the station. The police department had no leads. He'd been the best they had when he worked homicide, and it didn't surprise him when he listened to the voice mail message from Tangari asking that he come in for a meeting.

Dean Wood turned to face them. "These murders are hideous, disgusting. They're hitting the papers, drawing attention in ways we don't need. I don't have to tell you what that will do to the college. Tell me you have something. How far are you from catching this guy?"

"We're still in the process of going over interviews from witnesses of the last murder," Tangari offered.

Which was the way the cops told someone they had absolutely no leads at all. Well, Rafe didn't have to follow their bureaucratic crap any longer. He was his own man.

Standing, he stretched and met the Dean's gaze head on. "What I do know is sitting here discussing what we don't know isn't going to catch the murderer."

"Are you trying to tell me you have absolutely no leads?" A vein bulged in the Dean's neck.

"We're patrolling campus," Simpson told him. "Keeping an eye out for any unusual behavior."

"I don't see anything wrong with an increase in your patrol cars on my campus." Wood looked worried. "Just be careful in approaching my students. One wrong word gets out to concerned parents and I'll have a mass panic on my hands."

Rafe's phone buzzed and he pulled it from his belt, glancing at the number. He didn't recognize it but decided this was his perfect escape.

"I've got to run," he told the men staring at him expectantly. "Dean, I'll get with you soon. Let me take this call."

He let himself out of the office quickly, not giving Simpson a chance to protest. The man would be in touch. Rafe had no doubt. If they wanted to pick his brain, they would have to do it on his time.

Heading toward the stairs of the building that he knew all too well, he answered the phone before it went to voice mail.

"May I speak with Rafe Healy?" a woman asked.

"You've got him."

"Rafe? This is Emily." Her tone was quiet, sultry, stroking his insides to life.

"Hello, Emily." He lowered his voice, moving down the stairs quickly and heading toward the exit. "What's wrong?"

"Nothing really." She hesitated as if trying to figure out what to say next.

Rafe smiled for the first time that day. She wanted to see him. He hadn't made it into The College Pub this morning like he'd told her he would last night. She'd probably watched for him and now was checking up on him. Heading toward his car, thoughts of those large breasts in his hands was enough to stir his cock to life.

"Someone came in to have breakfast this morning," she began, again hesitating. "She asked me some odd questions."

"Like what?" Thoughts of her playing detective didn't sit well with him. At least now she called him with any concerns.

"Well...they were kind of sexual questions, like what kind of man I was attracted to and what I thought of having sex with strangers." Emily chuckled and at the same time he suddenly heard background noise, like she'd just started her car.

Getting in his own car, he checked the time. Possibly Emily was just getting off work.

"Where are you headed now?" he asked. He'd much rather have this conversation with her in person.

"I've got homework to do. I'll be home shortly."

"Give me the address."

She did and he told her he was on his way. After hanging up, his day suddenly seemed brighter. He needed to spend some time on the computer today, researching different names of some of the students he'd been keeping an eye on. It also had crossed his mind that his killer might not be a student, possibly a local who realized the campus environment was a well-stocked pool of luscious females.

Pulling into her parking lot, he didn't see her tan Buick. If she came from The College Pub, it shouldn't have taken her as long to get here as it did him. Pulling into the guest parking, he left his car and headed toward her building. Then he paused.

Ahead of him, the jock he'd seen sniffing around her before, Beaux Robinson, sauntered toward Emily's apartment. His research over the weekend had told him little about the young man. He wasn't involved in any sports, although he had the build. This was his second year, his grades were decent, and he'd graduate with his associate's degree in business at the end of the year. Other than the fact that he'd fucked a woman who'd been murdered minutes after he'd left her, there were no flags around him. Blame it on coincidence. Possibly. Usually coincidences turned into clues.

Rafe stuck his thumbs into his jeans pockets, slowing his pace. Beaux had disappeared into the alcove that led to the apartment doors. Rafe stopped before he could be seen. He didn't hear anything.

Snooping around in broad daylight wasn't an easy task. A young college girl walked out of the alcove, barely glancing at him while talking on her cell phone. There was no good reason to simply be standing there so he made his presence known. Walking past the girl, he approached Emily's apartment door. There was no sign of Beaux.

What bothered him even more was that there was no sign of Emily. This was her building, her apartment. There were two empty stalls right in front of where she lived. He shouldn't have to glance around the parking lot to see if she'd decided to park somewhere else, but he did anyway. She wasn't there.

Beaux shouldn't have just been able to disappear either. He walked to the other end of her building, where there was no parking, just the street. He didn't see any sign of the man.

"Fucking weird," he said under his breath and pulled out his cell phone.

Dialing the last number that had called him, it rang twice.

"Hello," Emily said, sounding either out of breath or like she was trying not to be heard by someone. Her voice was almost a whisper.

"Where are you?" He stood at the other end of the building now, looking both ways. There was no one on this side.

"Where are you?" she asked.

He scowled. "At your apartment, which is where you should be."

"Oh. Sorry. I'll be there soon."

He headed back to the alcove where her apartment was.

"You didn't tell me where you were."

"I ran a quick errand."

She wasn't telling him something.

"What errand?"

"I followed that lady. I'll explain when I see you."

"You did what?" Reaching her alcove, he stopped in his tracks when he spotted Beaux walking away from him toward the parking lot.

Now how the fuck did Rafe pass him without seeing him?

"She was weird, Rafe." Emily was still talking under her breath.

Every muscle inside him hardened. He clenched his phone, taking a deep breath to keep from telling her what a damn little fool she was for chasing after strangers—especially one she thought was weird.

"Get home...now," he said through clenched teeth.

"I will be there shortly." Her tone had a coolness to it that made him want to shake some sense in her.

She hung up, leaving an uncomfortable silence ringing in his ears.

Moving through the alcove, he caught sight of Beaux climbing into a small Taurus wagon, so unlike the kind of car he would picture a guy like him driving. The wagon was more like a family car. Beaux looked anything but the family man.

The guy started the car and then looked up, catching sight of Rafe. For a moment the two men simply stared at each other. Rafe felt the guy sizing him up, concluding Rafe was no match, and then with a smirk, backing out of his stall and taking off through the parking lot.

Quickly he made a mental note of the tag number and then headed toward his car. Finding a piece of paper, he wrote it down and then headed back toward Emily's apartment.

It still made no sense as to where Beaux had disappeared to when Rafe had first walked over here. There were no stairs. This complex didn't have second-floor apartments. Emily's door was in the alcove, with another apartment across from hers, which he assumed belonged to the young girl who had left when he'd first arrived.

He reached for Emily's doorknob, turned it, assuring himself it was locked. Staring at the door, at the knob, at the doorframe, everything in his mind screamed that there was something wrong with this picture. He turned, staring at the other door, and then looked back at Emily's.

Then he saw it. The small plate next to the doorknob, a simple piece that held the lock into the doorframe, was missing. Her door had been fucking messed with.

But how? How in the short amount of time that Beaux was in the alcove before Rafe had appeared could the man have fucked with her door?

A car engine sounded and he turned to look at the parking lot as Emily's Buick pulled into one of the stalls in front of him. Watching her climb out of her car, wearing tight-fitting jeans and a pullover shirt that hugged those large breasts, he gave her credit for knowing how to dress to show off every bit of sex appeal she had.

"Let's get one thing straight right now," she said, her expression hard with anger as she glared at him. "You don't tell me what to do. Understand?"

He'd deal with her tantrum later. "Let me see your key," he told her, holding out her hand.

Her mouth opened as she just stared at him for a moment. "Did you not hear what I just said?"

"Your door's been messed with, now give me your fucking key."

Those pretty blue eyes of hers turned an intense cobalt. Glancing at her door, she nibbled her lower lip. Silently, without saying anything, she held up her keys, separating her door key so that she held it with the rest of the keys dangling from her hand.

He took her hand, her cool flesh burning into his palm as he stared at her. Slowly slipping the keys from her fingers, he captured her gaze, watching the angry glare in her eyes fade into something more enticing. Her blue eyes darkened, warming, and then slowly, her tongue stroked her upper lip.

The act distracted him, but his protector's instinct was too strongly intact. Taking the keys, he unlocked the door, automatically holding out an arm to block her behind him.

"Let me check the place out first." He pushed the door open, entering the small living room area.

Noticing immediately that once again she ignored him, following him into her apartment and then shutting the door behind her, his attention focused on his surroundings, being able to only keep her somewhat behind him.

And even that was a challenge. Emily moved to the side, walking around the counter that separated the kitchen and living room.

"Everything looks normal," she told him.

Her door would need to be fixed immediately. Rafe locked it, knowing a good kick would send it flying open, then turned to give the living area his attention again.

Granted he wouldn't know if her things were out of place, but that wasn't what he was looking for. A serial killer often left messages, a gift, a promise of what was in store for the victim. Beaux Robinson had been in this apartment. Rafe hadn't witnessed it, but the rigged door and his unexplained disappearance left no other options of where he might have gone. Now to figure out what he'd been doing in here.

The layout was simple—a living room, kitchen, bath and bedroom. He walked through each room, giving most of his attention to her bedroom. She had a single bed. Women often had double-sized beds at least, yet Emily's bed was pushed up against the wall, a simple tan comforter hanging off the side, concealing what was underneath.

He went down on his hands and knees, lifting the blanket, and noticed nothing was underneath. Straightening, he turned, facing Emily who leaned against the doorway.

"What did you expect to find?" she asked.

"A person doesn't break into an apartment and then do nothing," he told her, looking around once again.

"Maybe no one broke in." She crossed her arms over her chest, pressing her ripe breasts together.

"I saw him." Rafe narrowed the space between them.

Emily took a step backward. "You saw who?"

"Beaux Robinson. He's in a couple of your classes, the jock who tried to get into your pants."

Her face paled as she looked up at him. "He was here?"

Suddenly she looked around her, glancing from one part of her room to another as if searching for something. Her fingers fluttered toward her face but then she put them on her hips, turning then shifting again and stroking her hair.

"Why does he scare you, Emily?" He took her arm, pulling her into the room.

At first she didn't fight him, allowing him to guide her to the middle of her bedroom. Then it seemed her thoughts became her own again, whatever fear that had clouded her face fading and being replaced with something more determined.

"He doesn't scare me. He's a jerk." Her jaw set but she still fidgeted.

Body language was everything. And the mere mention of Beaux's name made Emily very uncomfortable.

"Tell me about him."

"There's nothing much to tell." She finally met his gaze, those defiant baby blues taking him on. "He's just weird."

She wasn't telling him something, which made no sense. And he didn't like it.

Taking one of her hands, he brought it to his mouth.

"He's weird for coming on to you?" he asked, inhaling her scent as he spoke.

Her gaze dropped to her hand then slowly she looked up at him.

"He doesn't come on to me like you do."

"Good."

"The other night," she began then paused.

He couldn't help himself. Protecting her had him ready to spring, every muscle inside him hardening just standing in front of her. Whether it was the sultry way she carried herself, naturally yet with too much damned sex appeal, or her spunky and rebellious nature, he wanted more than just to ensure her safety. He wanted her to want him.

Scraping his teeth against her flesh, tasting her, inhaling her, made all the blood drain from his brain. Her lashes fluttered over those sensuous blue orbs as she caught her breath.

"The other night," she said again. "When you walked me to my car. He was there, hiding and waiting for you to leave."

"Damn it." He squeezed her hand, straightening as the previous night rushed through his memory.

Emily jumped, reacting to his sudden anger.

"He said he didn't want to disturb us since we were..." Again she paused.

Watching her as she replayed whatever happened in her mind, it was obvious her encounter with Beaux upset her.

"What did he do?" He wanted inside her. Not just his dick inside her, but inside her head, inside her mind.

"Nothing." She shook her head. "He held onto my door and gave me grief because I let you kiss me and not him. I took off on him."

"And then he shows up here." Well, the creep had just jumped up his list of suspects.

It bothered Rafe that Beaux didn't fit the profile of a murderer. But then, maybe he just didn't know enough about the man yet.

"There's no proof he was inside here." She looked around her, waving her free hand at their surroundings.

Rafe gripped her head, tangling his fingers through her hair. "Someone fucked with your door. I saw him walk into your alcove. When I walked to your door, he was nowhere to be found. I walked to the street. He wasn't there. When I turned around, I saw him heading toward his car."

He remembered the little Taurus wagon, a family car. He definitely would do more research on Beaux Robinson.

Emily stared at him while he spoke, her gaze moving from his mouth to his eyes. She just watched him when he finished talking, not saying anything. Her gaze lingered on him. Her free hand touched his chest, scalding him through his shirt.

She licked her lips and he knew she wanted him. Letting go of her hand, he cupped her head as she went up on tiptoes. Holding her, he took her mouth, diving deep into her heat with his tongue.

The enthusiasm she showed, her arms wrapping around him, her hands gliding up his back, pulling him closer as she gripped his shoulders from behind, unleashed the fire he'd barely been able to restrain.

Dragging his fingers through her soft hair, cradling her head, he moved her to deepen the kiss. A gasp escaped her, floating through him, bringing his need to a boiling point.

"I'm going to fuck you."

She better tell him "no" soon or there would be no turning back. Already his blood boiled, draining through his body, hardening his dick.

"Oh…God," she panted, her head falling back.

Running his hands over her slender neck, feeling her pulse rise against his palm, he knew she had to have him.

If he weren't careful, he'd ravish her so quickly that neither of them would get the full pleasure out of it. Emily would get better than that from him. Her body was created to be enjoyed, to give and receive all that sex had to offer.

He cupped her breasts, watching her eyelashes flutter over her eyes, her mouth move until her lips formed an adorable small circle.

"Look at me," he whispered, needing to see her pleasure.

Her tongue darted over her lips before she opened her eyes. Straightening her head, gazing at him under long lashes, the sensual blue of her eyes was like a deep warm pool. God. He ached to dive in and feel her heat.

"What do you want?" she asked, her moist lips barely moving as she spoke on a breath.

"Everything." And he did. Not just her body, but every bit of her.

"Then that's what I want too." She dragged him deep inside her with just her gaze.

His hands almost shook when he reached for the bottom of her shirt and slowly pulled it over her head. She lifted her arms, stretching before him like a cat. Large breasts, barely confined by a silky white bra, appeared before him. Full and plump, the sight of them sent his insides over the boiling point.

"Dear God," he breathed, cupping his hands over them.

He had to see them—all of them. Quickly he reached behind her and with a quick flick unhooked her bra and then watched like a child mesmerized with a new toy as her straps slipped off her slender shoulders.

White silk glided down her, revealing perfectly shaped, full, large breasts. Her nipples were large and puckered instantly in front of him. Brushing one of them with his thumb, it hardened further.

"They're perfect," he whispered, stroking her flesh and then reaching for the top button of her jeans. "I need to see the rest of you."

She took over the task, obliging as she unzipped her jeans and then slipped them down her narrow hips. She wasn't wearing any underwear. That knowledge had his cock throbbing so damned hard he could barely breathe.

Ripping his own shirt from his body and then about doing the same with his jeans, he needed flesh, needed to feel her softness against him.

With a few breaths, and her standing before him naked, waiting, he managed to regain control of his senses. A woman this beautiful wouldn't be someone he'd do just once and then thank for the good time. She was meant to be enjoyed again and again. The only way he could ensure that he'd keep her by his side was to make damn sure she enjoyed the moment.

At the same time, Emily would understand that fucking her wasn't something he took lightly. His days of whoring around had ended years ago. What he saw in Emily was something he planned to hold on to. She was so fucking beautiful, and her spunk and natural love for life appealed to him just as much.

"All I've got is the single bed," she said, suddenly sounding apologetic.

She shifted from one foot to the next, gesturing to it.

Rafe enjoyed how she suddenly seemed nervous. The last thing that would have turned him on would be if suddenly she showed incredible expertise in the bedroom.

He took her hand, stepping backward and then sitting on the bed. Her grin relaxed and she brushed her palm over his, stroking his chest as he leaned back against her pillows.

"I want to," she began, but then decided actions were better than words.

Moving between his legs, bending down so that she crouched before him, she ran her tongue over the length of his shaft.

"Oh, hell yeah," he breathed, his hands instantly on her head, holding her while he strained to keep his vision focused and watch her.

Streaks of red brushed through her brown hair as it fanned around her face. Her lips sheathed his cock, stroking him as she buried him in soaked heat. Then her tongue, daring and willing to explore, brushed up the length of his shaft. Rafe's head fell back on the pillow.

"That's it. Damn." He gritted his teeth, determined to enjoy her mouth a minute longer before pulling her on top of him. "Who the hell taught you how to do that?"

She moaned, the vibration pulsing through him, building the pressure that threatened to explode from him if he wasn't careful.

It took almost all his strength to not force her head back down when her swollen and moist lips left his cock. She stared up at him, running her tongue over her lips.

"Is that the way you like it?"

"I've never had it better."

She humphed as if not believing him and then crawled over him. Rafe was ready to pull her on top of him, but instead, she straightened, straddling him so that her pussy pressed against the tip of his cock. Running her fingers through her hair, she arched her back, let her head fall back and then slowly brought his cock inside her.

The heat and tightness of her soaked cunt was almost too much. Gritting his teeth, he grabbed her breasts, his hands not even fitting around the full, plump flesh. Her nipples hardened like beacons, pointing at him, while she worked inner thigh muscles, showing off a trim and in-shape body while slowly fucking him.

"God. Yes," she cried out.

He'd never seen a more beautiful picture. And sex had never felt so damned good. Just one more minute. He'd allow her that long to continue her slow and meticulous torture before he'd be forced to set the rhythm. If it weren't for the fact that her steady motions were about to undo him, he'd love the hell out of watching her fuck him like this for the rest of the day.

But damn.

"Rafe," she whispered, lowering her head for the first time, continuing her slow stroking of his cock with her pussy.

Her glazed-over blue eyes were full, bright. She lowered her hands, rubbing them over his hands that gripped her breasts and then squeezing. Instinctively, he tugged harder on her breasts and her pussy tightened while her mouth formed a puckered circle.

"Fuck yeah," she said on a breath, finally picking up the pace.

There was no way he could take it any longer. Every bit of blood and oxygen had left his brain, leaving him whirling with need to explode worse than any he'd ever experienced.

Grabbing her hips, pinning her in space, he thrust upward—hard.

"Shit," she screamed.

Her pussy was small, tight, untried yet so willing. He plowed into her humidity, taking all she offered and burying himself as far inside her as he could get.

"Fuck yeah," he growled, building the friction until the heat was more than he could bear.

"Rafe. Please." Her breasts bounced in front of his face while her fingers dug into his shoulders.

He had her right where he wanted her, holding on, trusting and giving him control.

"Now," he howled, releasing all the pent-up pressure, exploding as if he hadn't fucked in years.

Emily collapsed, her breasts better than pure heaven when they crushed against his bare chest. He wrapped his arms around her, enjoying the moment and needing to hear that he'd satisfied her too. She'd given him pleasure, taken the initiative, given what she wished, but it mattered that she'd enjoyed it. He waited, listening to her heavy breathing as she fought to catch her breath.

"You okay?" he asked.

"Mmm," she answered.

Rafe grinned. Answer enough.

Chapter Six

ဢ

Work the next morning seemed busier than usual. It didn't help that every muscle in Emily's body burned with the slightest movement.

"Order up," Carlos hollered, peeking over his counter as he placed several plates on the warmer.

"Thanks, Carlos." Emily dumped food off plates into the large trash can and then stacked dishes, wondering where Carlos' younger brother was.

None of them had time to be busboy and run their station.

"I got an order of hotcakes and french toast," Mary said, clipping the slip on the rotating holder where several other orders already hung. She nudged Emily, grabbing her next order. "You're making headway with that hot stud over there, aren't you?"

Emily didn't think she'd been that obvious. Hell. Since Rafe had arrived and managed to get a booth, she'd only managed to hit his table twice, refilling his coffee. They hadn't exchanged a word.

"Nothing serious," she said, shrugging.

Grabbing her order, she arranged several plates on her arm and then worked her way through the tables. There was no way she would talk about Rafe right now. They were too damned busy, and talking about him would just make her think about him more. And he was already tearing at her thoughts.

Not to mention, as sore as she was, just knowing he was in the third booth down, sipping at coffee while idly reading the newspaper, made her want him all over again.

"Good morning," she said, reaching the next table and placing the menu down.

The young woman looked up at her—the same woman she'd followed home the day before.

"It's real busy in here today." The woman didn't look like she liked that fact, staring around the restaurant nervously.

"It's been quite a morning." Emily managed her professional smile.

For the first time she regretted not sharing with Rafe the details of what she'd done before meeting him at her apartment. Sex with him had been so damned good that afterwards she'd been content to dive into her homework. Rafe had left her, returning later and insisting on fixing her door, adding a padlock for extra security.

Now, moving across the busy room and returning with coffee, she waited on the young woman, glancing down the row of booths to where Rafe sat, reading his paper. He glanced up at her, looking past the people in the booths between them, and met her gaze.

Emily looked away quickly. Those green eyes were intense enough to drown in. Focusing on the woman in the booth, her heart still beat a bit faster while need crackled through her like electricity.

"Just the coffee. And will you bring a cup of ice, please?" The woman stared up at Emily, never breaking eye contact.

Her pale blue eyes were almost frosty, like she'd led a hard life that had left her battered and empty inside. Hollowed cheeks and straight brown hair that needed brushing added to her unappealing appearance. The woman kept her hands in the pockets of a large baggy shirt, a shirt that seemed too warm for a day like this. If anything, her clothing hid well whether she was skinny or not—if it weren't for her gaunt face, it would be hard to tell.

"No problem." Emily maintained her smile, pouring the coffee and then hurrying to get the glass of ice.

The rush slowed, and she had time to clear several tables then slowed at the woman's table, once again ensuring her relaxed, friendly manner glowed. Too many years waiting tables had her swearing sometimes that she probably slept with this expression on her face.

"So are you a student?" she asked, refilling the woman's coffee cup.

"Oh no. The college is a terrible place." The woman leaned forward, her gaze dropping to the nametag on Emily's shirt. "Women who go to this school die, Emily."

The way she whispered, making her observation sound like a warning, chilled Emily's blood. She held the coffeepot in midair for a moment, staring at the cold expression on the woman's face that swam with hatred.

Deciding to try and keep this conversation alive for a moment, Emily nodded slowly. "I know," she said in the same tone the woman had used.

The woman nodded. "There's no way to stop it, you know. It will continue forever."

"What makes you say that?" she asked, her question automatic.

"You can't kill hatred. Believe me. I know. It's stronger than love." When the woman looked down, pulling her hand out of her pocket to dump ice cube after ice cube into her coffee, Emily stared at the disjointed part on her head.

"I don't know about that," Emily mused.

The woman looked up at her quickly. "It is. Don't ever think otherwise, or you'll be next. I tell you, it won't stop."

A sudden chill of fear almost made Emily shiver. The woman once again stared at her, not breaking eye contact. It seemed she didn't even blink.

"What makes you say that?" she asked, her mouth all of a sudden too dry.

This woman talked to her as if she had firsthand knowledge about the murders. Emily's heart beat so hard in her chest she fought not to keep the coffeepot she held from shaking. Just staring at her, it was as if she were looking into the most primal form of hatred that could possibly exist. The coldness in the woman's gaze was unnerving. Emily fought for a tactful way to learn her name, anything more about her that could help narrow in on finding the murderer. The woman sounded like she knew exactly who was committing the crimes.

"Because that's what Mother says." The woman brought her cup to her lips, sipping while glancing around at the other tables.

God. Maybe the woman was just a raving lunatic.

Emily nodded, at a loss as to what else to say. A few minutes later, the woman left, leaving two dollars on the table, the same as she did yesterday.

Shortly after that, Rafe brushed against her backside as she wiped down the booth table. "What are you doing when you get off work?"

His soft baritone had her insides swelling, pressure instantly peaking in her pussy. She balled the washcloth, turning to face him. He stood close enough that she'd have to edge around him, the booth pressing against her backside, just to gain space.

"Homework," she said automatically.

Although learning more about the strange ice-coffee drinking woman had crossed her mind.

"Then you'll be at your apartment."

She finally looked up into his face, noting his brooding expression matched the quiet demanding tone.

She shrugged, trying for indifference over his protective nature.

"That or the library." She didn't have a computer at her house and planned to do a check on the address she had after following that woman yesterday.

"You'll call and let me know where you are," he told her, then brushed a finger down her cheek, walking out before she could gather her breath.

The afternoon flew by, her homework consuming most of her attention. Thankfully, she'd not bothered to sign up for a thirty-minute block of computer time until later in the day. It wasn't hard to find a reverse lookup with the online phone directory. Typing in the address she'd written down the day before, she simply stared at the computer screen when the name, address and phone number popped up before her.

"Beaux and Darlene Robinson," she whispered, staring in disbelief. "She's his wife? His sister? What?"

A cold chill wrapped around her and she glanced around the quiet library, suddenly needing to see the peaceful reality surrounding her.

The woman disturbed Emily, something about her manner, the way she acted, not seeming quite normal.

Signing off the computer, she grabbed her things, thrust them in her backpack then stood, stretching, needing to get out of there. She had to tell Rafe about this.

After leaving voice mail, letting him know where she was, she had never heard back from him. Now she'd be calling him again. Albeit they'd had some damned good sex together, but she didn't want him to think she was chasing him. She didn't chase after any man.

Deciding on the wide flight of stairs, she hurried to the main floor. Somehow going back to her empty apartment seemed rather unsettling. Emily didn't want to be alone right now. Hurrying out of the library, she headed across the dark street, looking around her more than once, focusing on every dark shadow before she reached the large Union. There were at least a dozen students lounging and chatting in the large open area, surrounded by vending shops, when she entered. Collapsing into a comfortable chair, she stared up at the large television secured to the wall. A news reporter looked very serious as she reported the current events.

"And it seems a series of murders at the West Hills Junior College in Kansas City has faculty and staff more than concerned." The camera aimed its attention on the disturbing crime scene.

Emily's insides tightened and she couldn't look away from the screen as she listened to the report.

"The third murder in a week, police report no suspects in these unusual sexual crimes."

She stood too quickly and suddenly felt lightheaded. The murders had hit the news. At least now she had a good idea where Rafe probably was.

This time the darkness didn't even enter her mind as she hurried across campus. But she didn't head for her car. The camera angle focused on one of the nearby dormitories, and she hurried in that direction. Flashing red lights greeted her when she rounded the corner.

No way she'd get past that yellow tape marking off the crime scene. Glancing past all the emergency vehicles, she searched the crowd. She had loose bits of information. None of them really made sense, but maybe she'd see something here that would help.

"We need to clear this area," an officer announced, holding his arms out as he moved toward her and several other onlookers.

Emily moved on, walking along the sidewalk, doing her best to ignore the heavy shadows that crept away from the bushes alongside her. Watching the emergency workers move quickly, pushing a gurney toward the ambulance, black splotches stained the white sheet that was belted over a body.

Her stomach turned. Someone else was dead. Three murders since school had started. The killer was on a rampage.

She reached the end of the block and stood opposite the dormitory as she looked back toward the crime scene. No one stopped her from crossing the street, and she needed to head that way to get to her car, so she moved closer to the action from that angle.

Yellow tape surrounded the grassy area in front of the dormitory. Darkness shrouded Emily, the chill of the shadows making her shiver. Standing in shorts and her tank top, she crossed her arms, shifting her backpack strap on her shoulder. Ahead of her on the ground was a large black spot, white tape in the rough outline of a body adding to the gruesome sight.

A flash of light made her jump, her heart exploding in her chest before she realized a photographer had snapped a shot of the scene. There seemed to be more people standing around than there had a few minutes ago. She ignored their speculations and quiet whispers, her thoughts lingering instead on the strange woman she'd spoken to earlier today.

There's no way to stop it, you know. It will continue forever.

She shouldn't be focusing on the words of a crazy woman. Emily glanced around her, especially out here in the dark.

A vehicle screeched to a stop right behind her, and Emily moved further into the dark shadows, hanging heavy from bushes and the dormitory.

It wasn't safe in the darkness. Panic rose through her like nasty bile, making her stomach churn and her throat tighten while her mouth grew dry.

The darkness was no different than the light. Her mantra. Not to mention there were tons of people right alongside her. Nothing to be scared of now.

"Are you a student here?" a man asked.

He almost had her jumping out of her skin. She turned to see a tall lanky guy, his sandy hair cut short and his gaze alert as he took in the surroundings quickly.

"Yeah," she said, noticing an open notepad in his hand and another guy standing next to him, a camera braced on his shoulder.

The guy looked at her. "Murders like this got you thinking about leaving the school?"

She looked at him, aware the camera guy next to him adjusted his camera and aimed it her way. The last thing she wanted to do was be interviewed right now. Her mind already teetered on panic.

"I hadn't thought about it." Looking over at the van, she realized the station they worked for was from out of town.

"But there's been a handful of murders here since school started," the guy prompted. "All of the victims were nontraditional students."

His gaze traveled down her and she scowled. "And since I'm a nontraditional student, older than the average college student, I should be worried, huh?"

He had a pleasant smile and offered her a slight shrug. "Worried possibly, or maybe angry that your chance at an education could be hampered with fear over a killer."

"I'm not going to let some sick maniac steal my chance for an education," she said firmly.

The guy turned his head, breaking out in a full smile. "That's a take," he told the cameraman who nodded in agreement. Turning back to her, he pulled a card from his shirt. "What's your name, hon? You might see yourself on the morning news."

He offered her his card, but a hand thrust out in front of her, taking the card before she could reach for it.

"You're not putting her on the news." Rafe's anger filled the air as he pushed his way between her and the cameraman.

"Hey, man, she didn't tell me no." The reporter held his hands up, a slight smile on his face.

She was about to say that he hadn't asked her if she'd like to be interviewed. The words didn't get out of her mouth.

"She's telling you no now." Rafe grabbed her arm and almost yanked her off the curb into the street.

She struggled to keep up with his determined pace while keeping her backpack from sliding down her arm.

"Healy." Someone yelled at him, making his last name sound like an order.

Rafe turned, not letting go of her but slowing while a large man with a badge and gun attached to his belt made his way toward them. The cop gave Emily the once-over then let his gaze drop to the grip Rafe had on her arm.

"Did you talk to anyone who saw anything?" the cop asked, keeping his attention on Rafe's hand wrapped around her arm.

"Nothing." Rafe sounded disgusted. "It's like our killer is a fucking ghost."

"He's alive." The cop turned around, looking at the white tape covering the black stain that almost glowed with its eerie presence in the darkness. "Fucking bastard is going down."

"Yup." Rafe's grip tightened on her, even though his attention was on the crime scene as well.

His anger, his frustration at not being able to catch the killer, seemed to crawl through her from his touch. Glancing up at the hardness in his expression, staring at his profile outlined by darkness, he looked almost dangerous. In truth, she didn't know how dangerous he could be. Just now he'd displayed a temper, telling off the reporter and then manhandling her as he nearly dragged her across the street. But the flood of emotions, carnal and raw, gave her the sensation he'd tear into something without hesitating if he determined he was doing the right thing.

Suddenly Emily shivered, jerking her arm so he'd let go of her. His grip tightened.

"And with the media blasting this all over the place, we have less of a chance of him getting more stupid." Rafe pressed his lips together, still not focusing on her but damn sure not letting her go.

Staring at the tape that outlined a body no longer there. Imagining the amount of pain a person would endure to bleed that much, she realized that she'd edged closer to him. It was downright creepy that someone could do something like this to a person, and there were no witnesses.

Maybe seeing something like that happen would make you too crazy in the head to talk about it. She frowned, knowing without a doubt she'd be on the phone in a second if she had seen something that horrific happen.

"No one saw a thing?" She just found that impossible to believe. "You ever feel like you're missing something that is really obvious?"

Both men turned, looking at her as if she'd just said something incredibly ridiculous.

She stared at both of them then focused on the cop's nametag. R. Tangari.

"I mean, class just let out a bit ago. There would be people around." She pointed at the ground. "If no one saw that happen, maybe they didn't realize what they were seeing until the killer was gone?"

For some reason, the woman from The College Pub, with her ice coffee, popped into her mind.

"What the hell are you getting at?" Rafe asked, adjusting his grip and sliding his hand up her arm until he held her shoulder.

She'd never known a man with such a gentle touch that felt so dangerous.

"I don't believe you've introduced me to your lady friend," the cop said, crossing his massive arms over a thick barrel-like chest. For such a large man, he was very soft-spoken.

"Robert Tangari, this is Emily Rothmeier. I met her in one of my classes."

The cop stared at him blankly for a moment. "Oh yeah. You enrolled in school." Then looking back at her, he frowned. "So what are you getting at, Emily?"

"I don't know." She made a face at the godawful scene mapped out on the lawn across the street. "Just seems damn weird that someone would be murdered right there."

She was making a fool out of herself. Too many bits and pieces of information that were probably nothing ran through her head. The scream in the parking lot, Beaux leaving the apartment of that woman he'd fucked and then her getting killed, Beaux hiding behind her car until Rafe had left and the strange woman who liked ice coffee. There was nothing for her to grab hold of.

"Is there something you know?" Robert, the cop, spoke so softly it was unnerving.

Looking up at him, his expression didn't match his tone. Suddenly she was on the defensive and she didn't know why.

"If I knew something, I'd tell you," she said.

He nodded.

"Let me know about that autopsy report," Rafe said, letting his warm hand glide down her back.

Obviously he'd decided it was time to leave and that they were leaving together. Emily guessed she didn't mind an escort to her car.

"Emily," Robert said.

Rafe had just turned her toward the sidewalk and she looked over her shoulder at the cop.

"Watch out for him." He nodded to Rafe.

She almost smiled, assuming it was a joke, but Robert Tangari didn't smile. His expression and tone were serious. Turning from both of them before she could say anything, he walked to his squad car.

Rafe's hand was firm on her back as he led her back onto campus. "Why'd you come over here?" he asked.

"What did he mean by that?" she countered, looking up once again at his determined profile.

He didn't look down at her. "I'm not really a good catch."

Once again she realized she didn't know a damn thing about him—where he lived, where his office was, or how that cop seemed to know so much about him personally. Hell, she'd never even seen his car. Sure as hell said a lot about her seeing she'd already had some damn good sex with him. Guess that meant she knew one thing. He knew how to fuck.

Letting out a sigh, she scowled at the ground in front of them. His hand moved back up to her shoulder, draping his arm across her back as he walked alongside her, like they were a couple or something.

"You didn't answer my question," he prodded after a moment's silence.

"It was on the news. I went to check it out." There was no harm in admitting the truth.

"Do you always chase crimes?"

Ever since she was a child she'd loved being where the action was. And she never missed a good detective show or movie. Somehow sharing that with him probably wouldn't make him happy.

She shrugged. "Of course not."

Rafe grunted and something told her that he didn't believe her.

* * * * *

When they reached her car, he had left her panting after wrapping her in powerful arms and kissing her until she couldn't breathe. She hadn't seen him since.

Maybe that was best. After several days, a routine seemed to be forming, going to work, doing schoolwork, relaxing in her apartment, that was slowly starting to feel like home. More than once she wondered why he wasn't in class. And too often she woke out of breath, her dreams full of hot and wild sex with him. But, she told herself as she locked her car and hurried to work, it was definitely better to focus on a simple life than to chase after a dangerous detective.

Too bad simple lives were so boring.

"Don't you love chilly mornings?" Mary said in form of a greeting.

Emily loved the change of seasons, no matter which one.

"Make sure we got several pots of coffee going," Carlos yelled from the kitchen. "And put on a couple pots of hot water as well."

There was a clanging sound in the back room and then Carlos howled. Emily and Mary hurried back there, Emily stopping short when she saw Carlos, bent over with his hand on his back.

"Son of a bitch," he cried out.

"Are you okay?" Emily didn't know whether to touch him or not.

"Everything but my fucking back," he growled, his accent growing in anger.

"Go sit down for a minute." She grabbed the large trash bags he'd been hauling toward the back door.

Carlos started cursing under his breath in Spanish as he shuffled over to his small desk in the corner of the kitchen.

The trash bags bulged and had to weigh half a ton. Emily dragged them out the heavy back door into the alley where the dumpster was. It would probably turn out to be a gorgeous day. Storms through the night had lowered temperatures drastically, and tiny paths of water streamed down the middle of the alley, helping to clean out the smell that usually lingered back there.

Reaching the dumpster, she put the bags down and tossed back the large lid, which banged loudly when it hit the wall behind it. The sound echoed between the buildings. She glanced up and down the alley, a wave of unease suddenly rushing through her.

There wasn't a soul in either direction, just a heavy fog that made everything appear more gray than usual. Carlos had to have thrown away half the kitchen to make the bags so heavy. It took most of her strength to heave one of them over the side of the dumpster. It fell with a dull thud on top of the trash already in there. Unable to see over the top of the dumpster, she bent her knees, reminding herself to grab the other one properly. Last thing they needed was her to throw her back out too.

She missed and the damn bag fell to the side of the dumpster. Her shoes would be soaked through her entire shift. Doing her best to avoid puddles, she moved to the side of the dumpster and made a second attempt.

Throwing out trash shouldn't be such a chore.

Reaching for the lid, she stretched to make it stand and then let it fall with a terrific bang back over the top of the dumpster.

That's when she saw something move behind it and the wall. "What the fuck?" she breathed, backing up quickly and stepping directly in a puddle.

Someone darted out from behind it, almost running her down.

"God. You scared the crap out of me." And now her shoes were drenched.

The person, an older woman, glared up at her with cold blue eyes when she came to a quick stop so as not to plow into her. A large bag slipped off her shoulder, toppling to the ground before she could stop it.

Emily leaned over to help her pick it up and froze. Several large, cream-colored dildos rolled out of the bag.

"Touch them and you die." There was something weird about the woman's voice.

Emily straightened slowly, knowing there was no reason to be scared of a small older woman but at the same time feeling suddenly very nervous.

"I didn't mean to scare you." She managed to avoid the next puddle, moving toward the door while the woman picked up her toys.

If someone spills their purse, and very private items slip out, they usually hustle to return them, embarrassed and anxious to conceal what they would rather the world not see. The woman however, bent over slowly, gently fingering each dildo before carefully putting them back in her large bag. The strangest sensation rushed through Emily. It was as if she was proud to show them off.

Maybe they were like best friends to her. The thought of the older lady who seemed more dried up than a prune enjoying such large dildos made Emily's stomach turn.

The woman straightened, adjusting her bag over her shoulder and then brushing her hand over very short gray hair.

"Nothing about you scares me." Her expression was hard, almost evil.

"Glad you aren't scared then." Emily wanted to get back inside.

The woman gave her the creeps.

"Maybe you'd like one of these as a gift." She quickly pulled one of the dildos back out of her bag, aiming it at Emily as if it were a knife. "No. You would need to earn it first."

The fog seemed to part around the older lady, as if it didn't want anything to do with her either.

"Whatever." Emily ignored her furiously pounding heart.

Auburn didn't have many street people. And she wasn't accustomed to so many people that she didn't know. Not sure how to react to this strange character in front of her, she turned toward the door, more than willing to get her ass back to work.

The woman started chuckling, and Emily's hand froze on the doorknob. Turning to look at her, she watched her move down the alley with more agility than she'd guessed her capable of by her appearance. Before she'd reached the end of the alley, fog suddenly devoured her, making her appear almost ghostly.

Getting the creeps in daylight was stupid. Her hands shook when she hurried back into the safety of the restaurant.

Chapter Seven

ஐ

"She'd had sexual intercourse, but it appears he came outside of her." The mortician pointed with his gloved hands at the lower abdomen.

"Then he sticks a dildo in her?" Tangari asked.

Rafe rubbed his chin, feeling the several days' growth there as he stood over the desk staring at the group of pictures spread out before him. Tangari had held true to his word, calling Rafe in once the autopsy report had come back. More than likely what that meant was that Joe was as baffled by this case as Rafe was.

"And then he stabs her multiple times," Rafe finished for him.

No matter how many of these pictures he'd seen over the years, staring at mutilated bodies still made him sick to his stomach, pissing him off that he couldn't stop the monsters in the world. He stared out Tangari's office window, the gray buildings across the street almost the same color as the sky behind it. Fall was kicking in quickly.

"That seems to be the pattern he's following." Matt Hardister, the chief mortician from the crime lab, picked up the large plastic bag with the cream-colored dildo in it. "We've detected traces of both the woman's and the guy's DNA on these. But never any fingerprints."

Rafe didn't turn around to look at the dildo. "So we know he's using it on her after he fucks her, impaling her with it then stabbing her to death."

"Wonderful guy," Tangari muttered.

Rafe ran his hand through his hair. "I've been to every adult toy store in town. They all sell these. But no one has sold more than one to a customer at a time."

He'd also shown Beaux's picture to every employee in the stores he'd gone to. No one claimed having seen him before.

"Maybe he's getting them off the Internet." Tangari leaned back in his chair, clasping his fingers behind his head.

"Have you sent anyone down to talk to UPS or Fed Ex?"

Tangari nodded, closing his eyes. "Yup. Nothing."

Matt slowly began filing the pieces of evidence back in the cardboard file box. "The only thing I can confirm is that DNA matches on every murder. It's the same guy doing all of it."

Rafe already knew that. He didn't need crime lab verifying it but nodded anyway. He blew out a frustrated breath after Matt left.

"I think I'll head out too," he said, needing to clear his head of this whole mess for a while. Maybe he'd think clearer if he just let it go for a while.

"Where you headed?" Tangari stood, his massive frame making his chair squeak.

"I might do a drive-by to some of the residences of the guys I've made a list of." Or he might just stop by and see what Emily was up to.

He hadn't seen her all week. Maybe she'd be up for a drink, or just a good roll in the sack. Spending time doing something that had nothing to do with this case would probably do him some good.

"You still seeing her?"

Rafe met Tangari's hardened expression, perplexed how the guy always saw through a bad lie. He shrugged. "It's casual."

"Don't hurt her." He suddenly sounded like an overprotective father.

Rafe bristled. "I've never hurt a woman in my life."

Tangari raised an eyebrow. They had too much damned history together and the last thing Rafe needed or wanted right now was a fucking lecture.

"Just watch yourself." Tangari met him at the door, pulling it open and allowing Rafe to leave first.

He didn't look back at his old friend, his mood souring even further as he headed out of the station.

Pulling into Emily's parking lot ten minutes later, it dawned on him that Beaux Robinson was right in front of him. The jerk pulled into the stall that Rafe would have taken and parked. Rafe cursed as he circled around and took a spot in one of the guest stalls at the other end of the lot. Taking long strides across the lot, he stuffed his thumbs in his jeans pockets when he reached the back of Beaux's station wagon just as the young man got out.

Rafe wondered why Beaux waited until Rafe caught up to him before getting out of his car. If he got off on confrontation, Rafe had no problem giving him one.

"What are you doing here?" he said to the jock's back.

Beaux was possibly an inch taller than Rafe, broad shoulders and a firm body giving all signs that he worked out on a regular basis. He wasn't involved in any sports, or any extracurricular activities for that matter. The young man turned around, for a moment appearing distracted before he frowned.

"What are you, a cop?" he asked.

"Nope." But he used to be. Now he had the freedom to take on a suspect without red tape hindering his efforts.

"Then I guess it's none of your fucking business." Beaux turned from him.

Rafe grabbed his arm. Surprisingly, Beaux wasn't as rock hard as Rafe had expected. He was quick though and ripped his arm free, glaring at him.

"You can't get away with touching me like that." He took a step backward, not an aggressive movement.

Again not what he'd expected. Shame actually. Rafe wouldn't have minded kicking his ass.

"If you're here to see Emily," he said, going with his gut that Beaux was here to do just that, "you can get in your little car and leave right now."

"She doesn't want you," Beaux hissed, his eyes turning into angry slits. Balling his fists at his side, he looked like he was trying to suppress a nasty temper. "Emily doesn't want anything to do with you."

"Shall we go knock on her door and see which one of us she wants nothing to do with?" Rafe challenged him.

For a moment it looked like smoke would actually come out of the prick's ears.

"Fucking asshole," Beaux growled, his knuckles turning white as he fisted his hands but kept them at his side. "Women like her don't want old men like you. Get the hell out of here."

"I'll give you one minute to get in your car and leave," Rafe said quietly.

The young man shook with rage. At his age, if someone had pissed Rafe off that bad, he would have attacked first and asked questions later.

"Or what?" Surprisingly, the younger man took a step toward his car.

Rafe worked on a hunch. "Or I'll tell Emily the truth about you."

Beaux didn't say anything but wrinkled his brow, frowning. He seemed to be determining what truth Rafe might mean. For a second, it looked like his eyes rolled back in his head. His lashes fluttered down but then opened.

Remaining quiet, keeping his body relaxed, he waited for Beaux's next move.

Again Beaux moved toward his station wagon and then almost stumbled off the curb, reaching to stabilize himself as he leaned against his hood.

"There is no truth," he said, spreading the words out like it was an effort to speak.

Then he did stagger, moving backward. If Rafe didn't know better he'd say the man was drunk. Glaring at him, not saying a word, Beaux opened his car door and then almost fell inside. Instantly he gripped his steering wheel, closing his eyes and gritting his teeth until his face turned red.

Either he was ready to throw one hell of a tantrum, or something wasn't right with him. Rafe moved closer to the car door, watching as Beaux clenched his teeth and started breathing heavily through his mouth.

"Start the car, Beaux," he said quietly.

"Stop it. You can't make me do anything." Beaux didn't start the car. His hands remained glued to the steering wheel, white-knuckling it so hard it looked like he might rip it from the column at any moment.

Something wasn't right. Beaux looked straight ahead, as if tuning him out, never letting go of the steering wheel. He didn't move, didn't speak and didn't start the car. Rafe could've sworn he was staring at his murderer. Erratic behavior would fit the profile of this killer. All he needed was proof.

On a hunch, he grabbed the car door and leaned toward Beaux. "Why'd you kill them, Beaux?"

The man howled and pounded the steering wheel with his fist. "You're so fucking stupid. Stupid," he screamed. "I've never killed anyone."

Rafe had a perfect view of the interior of the car. A pine tree car freshener hung from the rear-view mirror. The back seat was clean, nothing on the floors that he could see. There was no dust on the dash, no CDs or cassettes lying around, no trash on the floors. He searched with his eyes, looking for anything that might incriminate him.

Slowly, Beaux took some deep breaths and then looked around him, showing strong signs of being disoriented. Rafe reached for his phone. Maybe questioning him further might be in order. But he didn't have any reason to call downtown. All he could do was rely on the fact that he didn't have to follow all the rules of a cop. It sucked he didn't have a tape recorder on him at the moment.

"You're the one who's stupid," he said quietly. "Everyone knows what you're doing and now you're busted."

"Fuck you," he screamed and then roared the station wagon to life, peeling out of the stall without bothering to close the door.

It was an act of God that he didn't take out any cars when he peeled out of the parking lot. Rafe grabbed his phone.

"Tangari," he said quickly when the cop answered his personal line. "Get a car on a silver Taurus wagon, late nineties model, Missouri tags, starting with Alpha, Beta George. It's Beaux Robinson and I just had a brief conversation with him outside Emily's apartment. He almost exploded and just peeled out of here so quickly you've got grounds to pull him over for reckless driving. Give him a good shakedown."

"Did he attack Emily?" Tangari asked.

"No. I stopped him before he got to the door. Our conversation was outside. I haven't seen her yet."

"I'll send a car to follow him, but you know as well as I do that if he obeys the rules of the road we can't pull him over."

Rafe cursed. "And you wonder why I'm no longer a cop."

Slapping his phone shut, he turned and knocked on Emily's door. It took a minute for her to answer, and when she did his breath caught in his throat.

She wore a long T-shirt, her legs were bare and she was barefoot. Her hair looked slightly tousled and he'd bet that damned T-shirt was all she wore.

"Is this always how you answer the door?"

"Every time," she said, sleep in her voice.

Stepping to the side, she allowed him to enter and then closed the door behind him.

"Get dressed," he told her.

"Is this your way of asking a lady out?" She ran her fingers through her hair, while her lashes hid her soft blue eyes. Her gaze traveled down him, her expression showing that she liked what she saw.

"When I ask you out, you'll know it."

Damn. More than anything he'd love to fuck the shit out of her. Taking her arm and turning her toward her bedroom, he cupped her bare ass. She didn't have anything on other than that T-shirt. Fuck. His dick got so damned hard from that knowledge he could barely walk.

Realizing that Beaux could have found her like this tore through him with a vengeance. The cops weren't going to do a damn thing until they caught the killer in the act. Just as when he was in the force, Rafe wouldn't—no, couldn't—wait that long.

They entered her bedroom and he tugged on her shirt. She hesitated, turning around to face him with a question in her eyes.

"You think you can just show up when you want and have a piece of ass?" she asked quietly, almost sounding wounded.

He puffed out a breath of air. "You don't know how bad I want to fuck you," he growled.

Her eyes grew wide. For a moment she stared at him, stepping backward, obviously thinking that she was getting laid at that moment whether she wished it or not. And in spite of his aggravation over the Beaux situation, a hint of amusement seeped through him when he saw her cheeks flush. Being stalked had its appeal to her.

Forcing that thought to a back burner quickly before it burned furiously through him, he picked up a pair of jeans crumpled on the floor.

"Get dressed. We're leaving."

"You're not making any sense." She took the jeans, frowning, and then sitting on the edge of her bed, slid them up her narrow legs.

He caught a glimpse of her shaved pussy before she pulled them over her hips and then stood.

"Why are you storming in here and then demanding that I leave with you?" She wasn't arguing with him, he'd give her that. Instead she slipped into her shoes and then tucked her T-shirt into her jeans.

"Beaux Robinson was just outside your door. I chased him off but we're going to find out where he lives."

"I know where he lives," she said quietly, not looking at him while she turned and grabbed her backpack.

"What?" He grabbed her arm, spinning her around to face him. "When have you been over at his house?"

"I haven't," she said, chewing her lip and suddenly looking somewhat guilty. "I did a search on an address when I followed that strange woman home from work the other day. I mentioned it to you."

"What's that have to do with anything?" He took her backpack from her, still holding her arm as he led them through her apartment.

"It's in my backpack. She's his wife, or something."

None of this made any fucking sense. He shut the door on her side of his Firebird and then slid behind the wheel. Emily pulled out a computer printout of a search she'd done from a common address search engine. He looked at the names and address listed.

"Beaux and Darlene Robinson." He handed the paper back to her and started the car. "And you followed her to this address?"

She nodded. "There's something seriously not right about her."

"Then she and Beaux must make the perfect couple," he scowled.

Slowing when they turned onto the side street, Emily pointed to the simple home, resembling most of the other houses on the block. Single-floor housing, more than likely two to three bedrooms, the neighborhood looked anything but where a college student would live. Beaux, in his Taurus wagon, and wife and home, gave all appearances of being a settled family man.

A family man with a secret of murder. Rafe couldn't ignore his strong hunch that he had his killer. Slowing in front of the house, they noticed there were no other cars parked nearby.

"There's no car in the drive," he observed, and no sign of the Taurus anywhere.

Emily stared out the window, her auburn hair waving naturally to the nape of her neck. Her T-shirt draped over slender shoulders and he'd grabbed her out of her apartment before she'd been able to put on a bra. The full roundness of her breasts pressed against her shirt, her nipples hardening while he watched. She knew he was staring at her.

"I'll be right back," she said quickly and jumped out of the car.

"What?" He jumped out just as quickly. "Like hell."

Grabbing her before she was halfway across their yard, he dragged her back to the main sidewalk.

"Exactly what do you think you're doing?" he demanded.

"I was about to ask the same of you." She shrugged her arm free of him, glancing quickly up and down the street. "You haul me out here. We might as well learn something. Just follow my lead."

She turned from him again, heading quickly up the walk to the front door of the house. Rafe scowled, unable to stop her a second time without making a scene in their front yard—not that the thought didn't cross his mind.

Emily tapped on the front door and then cleared her voice, not looking up at him but staring intently at the door. He'd give her this, she was brave—or foolish.

After a long minute, the door opened slowly, stopping at the length of the chain lock.

"What do you want?" a woman asked.

"Hi there. Remember me?" Emily smiled and sounded way too cheerful.

The woman stared at her and then looked up at him. He recognized her as the woman Emily had talked to a fair bit at The College Pub. It was hard to see much of her through the door, but straight brown hair fell around her face, and washed-out blue eyes hardened as she studied him.

"What do you want?" she asked, her tone quiet but guarded.

Emily shoved her hand into her jeans pocket and pulled out a set of keys. "You left these at The College Pub," she said, her tone still too cheery.

The woman shook her head. "They aren't mine."

"They aren't?" Emily frowned at the keys. "I was sure that they were."

"How did you know where I lived?" She made no attempt to open the door further but stared out, her eyes almost too big against her pale, gaunt face.

"I didn't." Emily shrugged. "When I was sharing my dilemma over the keys with this guy in one of my classes, he told me he was pretty sure I was talking about you. He gave me the address."

Emily smiled, looking very proud of herself.

"What man told you this?" Her voice dropped to a whisper, almost as if Emily's revelation terrified her.

"His name's Beaux. He told me you lived here. You sure these aren't your keys?"

"Stay away from Beaux," the woman whispered so quietly he almost didn't hear her, and then slammed the door in Emily's face.

"Well now. That's interesting." Emily looked up at him, looking suddenly very contemplative.

Rafe led her back toward the car, opening her door for her. Emily slid in willingly then turned to look toward the house.

"Rafe," she whispered, nodding with her head.

He turned in time to see a figure in the front window, holding the curtain back and watching them. The curtain fell, the person disappearing. He couldn't swear to it, but it didn't look like the woman who'd answered the door. But it was too small of a person to be Beaux.

"Shit," Emily said, staring ahead of her when he climbed in his side of his car.

"What?" Other than getting the sensation that the woman was scared of Beaux and not jealous that Emily mentioned him, he wasn't sure what had Emily looking white as a ghost at the moment.

Pulling away from the curb, he headed toward his place. Emily's nerve at confronting the woman living there had him worried. She didn't realize her vulnerability and seemed to think she could take on anyone. He had the urge to put a leash on her before she got her cute ass hurt, or worse.

"That woman in the window." Emily shook her head, as if trying to rid herself of an unpleasant memory.

"It wasn't the same woman who answered the door." He'd swear the woman in the window had short hair, not the long mousy brown hair that had fallen around the woman Emily had spoken to at the door.

Emily shook her head and then looked down at her hands which were clasped tightly in her lap.

"I think it's the same woman I saw in the alley this morning." Emily shuddered. "You think the lady at the door is weird. The whole family must be bonkers. If it's the same woman as the old lady I saw in the alley, she had a bag full of dildos."

Chapter Eight

ॐ

Just thinking about that old woman from the alley sent icy chills through Emily. She stared at Rafe's black shiny dash, the rich smell of leather and everything man filling the small area inside the car.

The car was as macho and dangerous as Rafe. It hugged corners, shifting easily as Rafe moved through traffic. More than a few minutes passed before she realized they were in a part of Kansas City she didn't know.

A sensation that she was losing control, having no idea where they were, rushed through her. She glanced at Rafe's hard profile, his large body somehow fitting perfectly behind the steering wheel of his hotrod.

"Take me home," she said quietly.

"We're going to my house." He didn't take his attention from the traffic.

Emily chewed her lip. Staring at him for a minute, his expression controlled, his features unreadable, a strange excitement surged through her at finding out where he lived.

Turning her attention to the road, she watched the large green signs go by overhead, putting them to memory although she was still clueless as to what part of Kansas City they were in.

"A gentleman asks before taking a lady somewhere," she mumbled, crossing her arms and leaning back some in her passenger seat.

"No one's ever accused me of being a gentleman before." He still didn't look at her and took the next exit.

Before long they pulled into a large gated community and Rafe pulled his Firebird under a carport with numbers above it. He didn't say anything as he guided her through the parking lot and across a small, nicely manicured yard. They entered a small patio guarded by a tall privacy fence and then unlocked the wooden door.

Darkness shrouded his town home, casting shadows over leather furniture and dark wall hangings of wolves that hung on the wall. There was power to the room, a masculine strength that sank through her, tightening her insides with nervous excitement.

The door shut behind her and then Rafe's hands were on her, gripping her shoulders with a firmness that matched the tough male aura in the room.

"I won't have you taking on these people like you can defeat them by yourself," he whispered in her ear.

Emily spun around, tearing herself from his grip. "I'm thirty years old," she hissed. "You think I've never had a stalker before? I know how to take care of myself."

He lunged at her, grabbing her before she could stop him and pinning her to the wall.

"Then free yourself," he whispered, his tone taking on a deadly sound.

"How dare you," she said, looking shocked.

She struggled and he pressed his body against hers. "Take care of yourself, Emily. Make me stop."

She fought him, twisting and turning. Her hair brushed over her face, blinding her. But her other senses were far from hindered. Powerful muscles touched her everywhere. His hard cock thrust against the softness of her abdomen. His fingers wrapped around her wrists, imprisoning her, stretching her arms. Her teeth clamped together as she put her heart into fighting him. Nothing she could do matched his strength.

Pulling her from the wall, he dragged her to the couch and tossed her on it. "Is this what you would do if you were attacked?"

No man had ever tossed her around like this. Rafe hadn't hurt her, and she wasn't stupid. His point was well made. Nonetheless, he mocked her. And damn it, that pissed her off.

As frustration pulsed through her, she stared at his pumped-up body, his breathing a little heavier than a minute before. Getting rough turned him on. The tingling rushing through her made her pussy pulse. Moisture clung to her shaved skin between her legs.

Adjusting herself on the couch, she stared into his smoldering gaze. "Now I guess it would depend on why I was being attacked?"

His expression didn't soften. The fire in his gaze seemed to make his muscles bulge further. Moving in on her, he leaned over her, resting a hand on either side of her against the back of the couch.

"Adrenaline rushing through a killer would be stronger than lust. You want my cock inside you." His tone was a harsh whisper, his gaze lowering to the rise and fall of her breasts. "A killer doesn't care about fucking you. They get off on taking your life. And that power is stronger than anything you're physically capable of fighting."

Glaring at him, she moved quickly, slipping under his arms and flying off the couch. "Don't insult my intelligence," she hissed, almost falling to her hands and knees as she bolted away from him.

Rafe lunged at her, grabbing the back of her T-shirt and pulling her backwards, tugging it free from her jeans. Keeping his hold, his other arm snaked around her, locking her to him.

"Don't chase after the killer by yourself." He leaned on her, almost overpowering her with his weight.

"I haven't gone anywhere that you haven't been. What are you worried about?"

He had her up against the wall again, his hand spreading over her waist. His fingers worked at the button of her jeans and within a minute tugged them down her legs.

"You," he whispered into her ear. "Promise me that you won't go chasing hunches of yours again without consulting me."

And then he would stop her from doing it.

Her jeans tripped her when she tried to move and she stumbled forward, his arm holding her up as her hands reached to stabilize herself on his table. His hand pressed against her back, under her shirt where his touch branded her skin.

"I don't need a keeper." Fighting to keep her voice level, Emily closed her eyes as he dragged his hand over her flesh, his fingers tweaking the sensitive nerve endings around her ass and then moving lower.

"Don't you?" His tone turned husky.

Strong fingers thrust against her moist cunt, sliding inside her. Pressure built with a quick intensity, stealing her breath. She sucked air in quickly, her reaction to him obvious.

Answering him, arguing with him, became impossible as he slowly started fucking her with his fingers. She needed to stand up to him, take on his carnal possessive side. Rafe would have her on a leash if she wasn't careful.

And that conversation would happen. But as long as he stoked the fire inside her, brought her to a smoldering mess of need, her thoughts fogged over too much to respond.

Rafe twisted his fingers inside her, knuckles scraping against flesh so sensitive, a fluttering rushed through her and she grabbed the table. Her breaths suddenly came too quickly. The scent of her sex filled her nostrils.

Slowly, he pulled out of her. For a moment she couldn't move. And she should have. His wet touch brushed over her ass.

"God," she cried out before she could stop herself.

116

Jumping, not prepared for his touch there, she found the power to move. But his hand clamped down on her back while those wet fingers circled nerve endings not accustomed to being touched like that.

"You've never been fucked in the ass?" he asked quietly.

"No." She shook her head, answering his question and trying to tell him at the same time that his touch was too intense.

He didn't stop but continued caressing her tight puckered hole, using her own cum to moisten the skin. Sensations rushed through her too fast, too hard. A sudden pressure streaked through her, too intense to control.

Crying out, she bucked against him. Rafe bent over and stroked her ass with his tongue, moistening it, teasing it, stroking those way too sensitive nerve endings. She plunged over the edge, need rushing through her while she experienced sensations too new and foreign to her for her to control or comprehend.

When he blew against the wet tortured flesh, she jumped then tripped over her jeans balled around her ankles. Unable to stop herself, she almost fell over the side of the table.

"Come here," Rafe whispered, grabbing her.

"You can't trap me like this." And she meant more than her jeans immobilizing her.

The sudden memory of the cop from the other night, Robert Tangari, warning her to be careful around Rafe came to mind. Rafe had told her he wouldn't make a good catch. His aggressive, dominating nature needed curbing. She was always up to a good challenge, and as she stared into those lust-filled eyes when he pulled her to him, seeing something darker, it challenged her.

"Trap you?" The dark depths of his soul should be terrifying. They came forward, penetrating through her. "I don't think I have to trap you."

Add way too confident to that list of character traits he was displaying.

Slipping out of her shoes and then kicking her jeans off, she let him continue holding her arm while moving a chair next to the table and sitting in it. Her oversensitive ass and soaked cunt pressed against the cool wood and she adjusted herself quickly, catching her breath.

His cock bulged against the restraints of his jeans, and she ran a finger along its length, feeling satisfied pleasure when it jerked against her touch. Rafe sucked in a breath and she looked up to see him looking down at her, watching her with a more intense gaze than she'd ever seen in a man before.

There was a certain appeal about a man dangerous enough to fear but enticing enough to stimulate her into wanting to take him on, challenge him, discover the source of the darkness that brooded deep inside him.

"Then what do you have to do?" she asked, intentionally running her tongue over her upper lip.

A sense of power rushed through her when he watched the act.

He didn't answer her. She'd pushed into that space that she guessed he didn't want her to see. There was a dark side to Rafe Healy, a side she'd been warned about. It excited her. He didn't want her investigating anything without his knowledge, but she couldn't leave it alone.

Popping the top button of his jeans undone, she slowly unzipped his pants then stopped, making no attempt to undress him further. Instead she let her fingers linger, once again stroking his swollen shaft. His quick intake of breath fueled her fire. Moisture grew between her legs, making it hard as hell not to pull that cock out and demand that her cravings be satisfied.

"Must you always control a situation?" she challenged, looking up at him while pressing her palm against his cock.

"Only when the situation needs controlling." He grabbed her hand, pulling her to her feet and then shoving his jeans down.

His cock jumped to life, eager and demanding. Her body responded, needing him inside her.

When he tugged on her arm, forcing her toward the table again, she grabbed his cock, gripping his throbbing shaft hard enough to make him stop moving.

"Emily," he growled.

Maybe he'd never been challenged before. Possibly no other woman had dared take him on, seeing the aggressive side of him and worrying it might be too dangerous a place to enter.

He'd already guessed that danger excited her.

"Sit down." She pointed to the chair.

When he didn't move, his expression hardening while his gaze devoured her, she tugged on his cock, getting his attention.

"Sit," she whispered, deciding by his intense expression that making her demand too severe would get her nowhere.

He didn't let go of her arm when he took the chair, pulling her to him when he sat.

"Take your shirt off," she whispered, this time because she couldn't get her voice to master anything above the slightly uttered words.

A slow half-grin spread over his mouth, amusement not quite taking away the dark brooding gaze that was sending her over the edge. At any moment he could pounce, she sensed it, felt it while every nerve ending in her body was on the verge of exploding.

Letting go of her forearm, Rafe pulled his shirt over his head, giving her an eyeful of thick solid chest muscle covered with dark coarse hair. His abdomen was taut, firm, and led the way to the dark small curls that covered his groin. Her mouth went dry when her attention locked on his cock, hard and smooth, raised straight up, ready for her to slide down on.

Quickly removing her own shirt, she straddled him, resting her hands on his shoulders while positioning herself over his swollen cock head.

"Is there something you want?" Rafe grabbed her hips, holding her so that she couldn't sheath his cock.

"I thought it was what we both wanted." She was about ready to explode. His cock brushed against the entrance of her pussy.

The swelling pressure growing inside her while he held her, suspended, just above his cock, made her ache to have him inside her.

He didn't take his gaze from hers when he pushed down on her hips—hard. His cock slid inside her easily, filling and stretching her as it seemed to race to fill her. The impact of him taking her like that sent the pressure inside her exploding into millions of pieces of charged energy. The energy rushed through her, tearing at her, breaking the dam that contained the pressure and sending it spilling throughout her.

"Holy shit!" She dug into his shoulders, arching her back as her head fell back.

Adjusting her position didn't help. Rafe reached a spot inside her that no man had touched before. The initial contact sent her over the edge, falling, spilling through her so that all she could do was hold on and endure an orgasm that almost rendered her unconscious.

"That's it, sweetheart." His voice soothed, yet showed her the intense satisfaction that surged through him that he'd once again taken over the situation.

Lifting her, he dragged himself almost completely out of her before shoving again against her hips and forcing her to impale him. His cock was so hard, so forceful, she could barely keep her legs from giving out and collapsing on him completely.

And that hadn't been the plan.

"I want to be in charge," she managed to say, digging hard into his shoulders with her fingers as she clamped her teeth together.

Determination warred with the incredible sensations that he'd sent plunging through her.

"I'm very aware of that," he said, sounding calm enough to get her dander up.

"Move your hands." She managed to take her hands off his shoulders and grab his wrists.

Muscles in her legs burned as she held herself over him, straddling him but keeping herself above him so that he wasn't completely inside her cunt. And that in itself was almost more torture than she could endure. Her heart pounded while muscles inside her twitched, craving rushing through her so hard she almost broke—almost let him do as he pleased.

He moved his hands quickly enough that she let go of his wrists and he grabbed hers, bringing them up between them. She used his strength, leaning into his forearms that held her weight without letting her lean forward too far.

"Yes," she sighed, finally able to ride him the way she wanted, the way she needed to.

Rafe watched her, green eyes not blinking while his dark eyebrows made his gaze appear deadly. His grip strengthened around her wrists and she balled her hands into fists as she continued riding him.

That thick, long cock of his stroked her insides, cum soaking both of them as she worked her leg muscles, feeling them burn and not caring. Nothing had ever felt better or relieved a stronger itch. She was sure of it.

Closing her eyes and relaxing, leaning into his arms that remained hard and pinning her wrists together, she enjoyed how damn good he felt.

"Do you feel how soaked you are?" Rafe asked, still not moving as she'd willed.

His cock twitched inside her, and his leg muscles hardened like stone. There was no way he'd hold out much longer. The way her arms were pressed together, her wrists in his hands, she knew her breasts had to be more than an eyeful for him. Squeezed together between her arms, her nipples hard and her breasts swollen with an ache that pulsed throughout her.

"Uh-huh," she said, blinking her eyes several times, trying to clear her vision and study his expression.

"That cum will soak your ass, make it ready for me."

That cleared her vision and tripped her rhythm. She stared at him, his sober expression, the thick haze of desire that made his eyes look like deep green pools. As she watched him, his cock swelled inside her. Lowering herself over him, forcing him to sink deep inside her, she paused at his words.

"I've never done that before." Nervous energy rushed through her while his cock twitched deep inside her.

Without warning, Rafe stood up, lifting her off him too fast for her to respond. With quick strides, carrying her, he moved through his town home, up the stairs and then down a short hallway.

"What?" She tried to adjust herself in his arms, her cunt burning, throbbing as his hard cock pressed against her while he moved. "What are you doing?"

They entered his bedroom and she barely got a chance to look around before he dropped her on his bed and then was on top of her.

Lifting her legs, he buried himself deep inside her again. Her ankles rested on his shoulders and he adjusted himself, hovering over her on his hands and knees as he began fucking her.

"You had your time to be in charge," he told her, his tone rough as he picked up the momentum.

"Rafe." That was all she could say.

Hell, she couldn't think.

Tension erupted inside her, taking her over the edge, and still he didn't relent.

"God…damn." The words tore from her lips.

She shook her head from side to side, reaching out for him, clawing at the air while he fucked the living shit out of her.

He played rough, giving adrenaline free rein, pounding her pussy, creating so much friction that fire burned inside her. He hit the spot, that special spot that she'd just recently learned she had. Hitting it again and again while lights exploded in front of her eyes. Moisture poured free from her.

And still he didn't let up. Riding her hard and with so much intensity that she couldn't focus, all Emily could do was hold on, pray she didn't pass out from the way he fucked her.

God. Would she ever be able to think straight again?

"Rafe. Oh God."

A slow growl started deep inside him, vibrating through his body so that she swore she felt it inside her. Barely able to focus on him, she fought to clear her vision, aching to see his face when he came.

His eyes were closed, and he threw his head back, corded muscles bulging in his arms and stretching across his chest as the growl turned into a roar.

He exploded inside her, soaking her quickly so that she felt his hot cum seep out of her, soak her ass and inner thighs.

"Damn it," he said through clamped teeth, and slowly brought his head forward until he captured her gaze.

"You're not bad," she managed to utter, feeling a need to lighten the emotions she suddenly felt.

No one had ever fucked her like that. And she'd have to hear a damn good story to believe that Rafe fucked many women that way. Warmth spread through her and it wasn't from the fire that continued to smolder between her legs.

His chuckle was deep, dominating, while he gave her an incredible look of satisfaction.

For a moment it seemed the darkness she'd seen in his eyes before had left. But when he pulled out of her, giving her one more look before moving to lie next to her, she saw it return. Some deep, raw emotion, dark and dangerous, lingered behind his gaze. It excited and made her nervous at the same time.

"I meant what I said earlier," he told her, his tone still gruff as he slid an arm underneath her neck and pulled her to him.

His heart was a heavy thudding in his rib cage as she rolled to her side, placing one hand on his coarse chest hair and nestling her head against his shoulder.

"You're going to tell me where you go, or you're not going to leave my side." His grip on her was predatory, pinning her to him, as if to show her how easily he could carry out his words.

There was nothing she could think of to say that would satisfy him, and she was too sated at the moment to argue. Closing her eyes, she listened to his strong steady breathing and slowly drifted to sleep.

Chapter Nine

ა

Rafe hadn't sat in on any of the classes in a week. But tonight, taking the desk he had before at the back of the classroom, his gaze drifted from the back of Emily's head to the other students in the room.

The American literature class was required for many students, and the classroom was good-sized, designed to accommodate the large enrollment. There was a mixture of young students and older ones, those who had come back to finish their degree or were taking a shot at college for the first time.

Several women managed to glance his way, showing signs of interest or simply sexual curiosity. It wasn't something he was unaccustomed to, but until recently, very recently, he'd sworn off women. Other than casual sex with a willing stranger, and they'd been few and far between, he'd realized a long time ago that he wasn't the settling-down type.

If a woman got under his skin, he cared too much. Tangari had told him once that he was a kickback to another time, a time when men were men and women were women. That hadn't made a damned bit of sense, but whatever the reason, as soon as his heart got involved, every woman he'd had a relationship with took off running. They left him as quickly as they could, usually with a door slamming in his face and a few choice words screamed at him.

Emotions he'd thought he'd killed, feelings he'd sworn he would never feel again, seemed to be surfacing. Damn Emily Rothmeier anyway for getting under his skin like that. And so quickly. Her fiery attitude, that damned sexy body of hers and the way she took him on—no other woman had pulled such primal reactions out of him so quickly.

"Remember to get your research proposals in to me," the professor was saying as sudden noise filled the room.

He hadn't been paying attention and the class was over, quick movement and chatter filling the room. Rafe stood and realized Beaux Robinson stood talking to Emily. Anger surged through him at the young punk's nerve. The guy had his back to him, as if he hadn't even noticed Rafe was in the classroom.

Moving around several students who gathered notes and books together, he saw her face. She looked up at Beaux, smiling and answering something he'd said to her. Before he could get to her, she'd written something down and handed it to Beaux.

"Emily." He reached her side and met Beaux's gaze, which switched from cocky to hostile so fast it was unbelievable.

Beaux looked away from him. "I'll talk to you soon," he told Emily and sauntered out of the room.

"What were you doing?" he asked, taking her backpack from her and then placing a hand on her back to guide her out of the room.

"I gave him my phone number." She didn't look up at him, her tone sounding light enough that he knew she was gearing up for an argument.

"I warned you about him." He guided her in the opposite direction that most of the students headed, taking the staircase at the other end of the hallway toward the street.

"And you suspect him. I agree there's something odd about him. If he's the killer the only way to prove it is to catch him in the act." She looked up at him. "And stop him before he kills again."

"You're not going to be the bait." He knew exactly what she had in mind when he looked into the determined glow in her face.

She got quiet when they left the building, not arguing or challenging him like he'd expected. If anything, she seemed to quicken her pace, keeping a tight grip on his hand as they moved, cutting across the dark lawn in front of the building toward his car he'd parked on the street.

"Is that him?" she asked, her voice a soft whisper.

He looked down at the way she'd wrapped her arm around his and held his hand firmly. Her palm was damp and her eyes wide in the darkness. No matter how tough she liked to present herself, Emily was nervous out here at night watching a possible killer stroll down the sidewalk less than half a block ahead of them.

"Yup." He searched the street for the Taurus that Beaux drove but didn't see it. He slowed their pace, deciding they'd follow him to see where he went.

A cool breeze had settled in after the day had reached a balmy warmth. The mixture of airs now resulted in a fog settling in, making it hard to determine figures if they got too far away.

Beaux walked with purpose ahead of them, leading them toward the small bar at the end of campus.

"Up for a beer?" Rafe asked, adjusting her backpack over his shoulder and then brushing his fingers over the small gun fastened to his jeans at his hip.

"I'm up for seeing what Beaux is up to tonight." The sudden excitement in her voice had him looking down at her.

"Remember what I said about chasing after people," he warned her.

She looked up at him, noticeably relaxed as her auburn hair glistened under the bright streetlights.

"But I'm not alone. My protective guard dog is right next to me," she teased, grinning up at him easily.

"I'll show you protective guard dog," he growled.

Waiting for several cars to pass in front of them, they crossed the street well after Beaux had entered the bar.

Knowing the front door was the only way for customers to leave and enter the bar, Rafe suggested they sit out on the front deck, choosing a bench that was somewhat sheltered by dark shadows.

"What are you all drinking tonight?" A cheerful young waitress, barely looking old enough to serve alcohol, walked up to them. When she got closer, her grin broadened. "Hey, Emily."

Emily grinned as Mary, the young waitress she worked with at The College Pub, let her gaze linger on Rafe for a moment before giving her a knowing wink.

"Hi, Mary. I didn't know you worked here too."

Mary shrugged, balancing a round tray against her hip. "Just a couple of nights a week."

"How about if you bring us a pitcher of whatever you have on draft," Rafe suggested, leaning back against the bench and spreading his arms over the back of it.

He recognized the young girl from The College Pub. She looked like at least half the girls on campus—and he did mean girls—with her picture-perfect, almost too skinny young body. She gave them both an easy smile and hurried off to get their beer.

Staring for a moment up at the sky, too many nearby lights prevented him from seeing any stars. Although by the looks of the hazy night, he doubted there would be any stars or moon out this evening.

"Do you need anything from your apartment before we head back to my house later?" he asked, feeling Emily relax next to him.

Glancing over at him, she straightened, her hair brushing against his arm as she looked at him.

"I'm not staying the night with you," she said firmly.

"You're not staying alone in your apartment when that asshole knows where you live," he said simply. This wasn't a discussion.

Mary brought them their pitcher and two chilled glasses. A handful of students bounded onto the deck, laughing and suddenly filling the quiet night with easy conversation. Rafe pulled a bill from his pocket, telling Mary to keep the change, and watched behind her as two women possibly his age entered the bar.

"Looks like we'll be busy for a while," Mary said, sounding like she was up for it. "Holler if you need anything else."

Rafe ran a finger over Emily's shoulder, getting her attention after the people on the deck had settled at tables, their conversations lively but not intrusive. No one horned in on their shadowed corner at the edge of the deck.

"Rafe," Emily said with a sigh. "I just don't know you well enough to start spending the night with you all the time."

Her words should have him sighing with relief. For years he'd searched for a casual relationship, a decent lover who wouldn't get inside his head.

"Then get to know me," he heard himself saying. "Ask me anything."

"Why aren't you a cop anymore?" she asked him, not missing a beat.

He stared at her for a moment. "What makes you think I was a cop?"

"I'm not such a bad detective," she said.

"I left the force five years ago," he told her, glancing toward the door when it opened and a pimply college boy walked outside.

Emily looked that way too, letting out a breath when it wasn't Beaux. "Why'd you leave?" she asked.

Rage stared at her. This wasn't something he discussed with anyone.

"Tell me," she whispered.

"I left so the force could save face and to avoid possible charges of murder."

Her jaw dropped and she stared at him, her gaze shifting as she searched his face. His conscience was clear, and he'd be damned if those old ghosts would taunt him now. Remaining relaxed, he'd let her form her own opinions. It wouldn't change anything today. She was going to go home with him.

The door to the bar opened and Beaux walked out, his arm wrapped around a woman. It was hard to see her with his massive frame in the way. Beaux didn't look in their direction but focused on his conquest for the night, bounding off the deck with her and across the street.

Emily jumped to her feet. Rafe stood and took her arm. "Go inside and wait for me," he told her. "Your friend Mary is working in there. Chat with her and don't leave."

She looked up at him, surprised. "Like hell. I'm going after him with you."

"There's no time for argument here."

"You're right." She narrowed her gaze on him. "If you're going to spend all your time bossing me around and treating me like some half-wit bitch, then we might as well part ways right now. We're equals or we're nothing."

Arguing with her right now would cause him to lose Beaux. And he wouldn't let that happen. No more women would be killed if he could stop it.

"We'll discuss this further later," he growled at her, heading off the deck and keeping a firm grip on her arm.

"Works for me," she said, easily keeping up with him.

Beaux and his lady walked arm in arm a good half-block ahead of them. When they disappeared down the steps toward the parking lot, Rafe cursed. His car was parked here on the street and it would take too long to drive around campus to the exit of the parking lot. He'd parked his car on the street when he'd seen Beaux's Taurus parked there.

"I can drive your car to the entrance of the parking lot," Emily suggested, obviously seeing the same dilemma he did. "Wait in the parking lot so you'll know what car they get into."

She held her hand out for his keys. He had to agree he'd rather be the one waiting in the dark alone than having her do it. Pulling his keys from his pocket, he handed them to her.

"Can you drive a stick?"

She rolled her eyes at him and then turned and jogged across the street. He enjoyed the view for only a moment before heading for the stairs, keeping to the dark shadows as he watched Beaux and the woman reach the bottom.

Fortunately, the two of them seemed to be enjoying some active foreplay already and didn't notice him. Moving slowly through parked cars, ready to duck if either of them turned, Rafe watched Beaux fondle the woman.

They reached a car parked in the middle of the lot, surrounded by other cars, and she turned, leaning against it while wrapping her arms around Beaux's neck and then leaning back when he towered over her, kissing her.

Lights beamed across the lot when Emily pulled into the lot in his Firebird. He moved through the parked cars until she saw him. Slowing, she put the car in neutral, pulled the emergency brake then climbed out when he opened the car door for her.

"Where are they?" she whispered. There was a sense of urgency in her voice.

"Over there. Get in." He guided her around his car and opened the passenger door, waited until she sat, then closed her door and hurried to the driver's side.

Then parking on the edge of the lot, backing into a stall, he cut the lights and let them fade into the darkness.

"I don't see them. Where are they?" she asked.

"Over there."

But they weren't leaving the lot. Instead, Beaux seemed to be willing to fuck the woman right there between the cars. And surprisingly, the woman seemed to be getting into it as well.

They weren't by any of the lights that flooded sections of the parking lot. In the darkness, Rafe kept his gaze on them, worried if he looked away he might not be able to see them again. They were two dark figures, silhouettes in the night, moving and swaying in each other's arms in the dark and quiet parking lot.

It had barely been a month since the woman had been murdered in almost that exact same part of the parking lot. He questioned the intelligence of the woman for allowing Beaux to fuck her right there alongside her car.

"If he does something to her," Emily whispered, although there was really no reason for her to keep her voice down inside his car, "I mean, if he stabs her or something, we're too far away to keep him from killing her."

"Part of the job is learning how to wait," he told her as a sudden flashback hit him.

It seemed like another lifetime when he'd yelled at his partner, knowing that sitting and waiting, watching, would mean yet another murder. Ignoring his orders, disregarding the captain when he'd screamed at Rafe over the two-way in their patrol car, Rafe had rushed into the night, determined to save a woman's life. Disregarding orders had become somewhat of an issue between him and his captain. And he'd already been written up once.

None of that had mattered to him when he tore out of the squad car, ignoring his partner yelling at him and the screaming of his captain through the radio.

It had been a cold night, and Rafe still remembered seeing his breath when he'd entered the abandoned warehouse in a part of Kansas City that most cops wouldn't walk at night.

He'd walked into a sight that would have made some men larger than him faint. The woman had been tied to the wall, naked, clamps on her nipples and a ball stuffed in her mouth. Leather straps were tied around her face, around her hair, and secured behind her head. Similar leather straps were wrapped around her wrists and ankles, securing her to railroad nails that had been stabbed into the wall.

Rafe had simply stared for a moment at the large red welts that stretched across her creamy white skin. Her long black hair fell to her ass, some of it streaming over her breasts and brushing against her flat abdomen. Under different circumstances, it would have been a scene hot enough to make his dick hard.

The Master beating her with the long bullwhip was wanted for murder. And more than likely she would be his next victim. Sitting and waiting to catch him in the act of killing her would have meant she would die so that they could put him behind bars. Rafe wouldn't accept that.

He'd caught the man, who wore nothing more than leather pants, with his cock bulging when he turned around, off guard, startled at the young cop who'd suddenly violated his private session.

"Who the fuck are you?" the man scowled, still holding his whip in midair, now looking like he might try to strike Rafe with it.

Rafe had been young, nothing more than a punk with a temper who'd thought he could make a difference becoming a cop. But his attitude got him in trouble too many times, the bureaucratic red tape he was forced to jump through pissed him off one too many times.

And he remembered exactly what he'd said too.

"Your worst nightmare." And Rafe had pulled his gun on the guy. "Put the whip down and get down on your knees."

The man had laughed at him, which had pissed him off even further.

Hurling the whip through the air, he'd forced Rafe to jump to avoid being hit by the lethal-looking weapon. And that had been enough for the murderer to run, disappearing, leaving Rafe with the dilemma of whether to chase him down or help the woman whimpering, tied to the wall.

He remembered that he'd called for backup. At least he had that much to back himself with. He'd used his cell phone and immediately told his partner where the man was heading.

But his night had gone downhill from there. He'd been young, stupid, and his temper was more in check these days. He knew enough now to see the warning signs when his temper started raging through him.

Taking his time, freeing the woman, and even giving her the shirt off his back, the stupid bitch wouldn't give him any information.

"I won't turn in Master," she kept mumbling, a fever rushing through her from the extent of damage from the whipping she'd just endured.

He cringed remembering how he'd gotten in her face, telling her she was protecting a criminal and that in itself could land her in jail. His captain had shown up and had been the one who'd called the ambulance. Rafe had simply yelled at her until ordered out of the building.

The woman had died an hour later in the emergency room, having bled to death from the small knife that had been inserted inside her pussy, causing internal damage that Rafe hadn't noticed. It had taken a few months but that night had come back to haunt him, the family finally tracking down the truth and then wanting to press charges against the police department for allowing her to die and not taking quicker action to ensure that she lived.

Rafe had resigned shortly after that, knowing that doing so would help the force save face and keep him away from possible charges for murder. Life had been a lot better since then. At least now he was his own boss, and the only one who could yell at him for his fuck-ups was him.

Rafe brought himself back to the present when he realized the shadows he'd been staring at had parted. Beaux took off across the parking lot and then jogged up the side of the hill, not taking the stairs.

"Oh shit! No!" Emily cried out, opening the passenger door. "It's just like last time."

She hurried out of his car, shutting the door behind her.

"What the fuck?" Rafe jumped out of his side, managing to intercept Emily and take her down, the two of them hitting the hard asphalt with loud grunts.

"It's going to happen again," Emily said, instantly crying.

"He left her. What the hell are you talking about?" He pulled her to him, quickly moving to his knees.

Emily struggled furiously in his arms, forcing him to use a good amount of his strength to keep her pinned to him until finally she quit struggling.

"I saw it. I didn't know I saw it. And I didn't do anything about it." She was crying and speaking through sobs and not making one fucking bit of sense.

A scream tore through the air, and Emily jumped, also screaming so loud it pierced his eardrums.

"Rafe. Stop it. She's going to die." Once again she struggled in his arms.

This time he pulled her to her feet, stabilizing her before darting across the parking lot, his gun pulled.

"Rafe. God," Emily cried out from behind him.

He reached the place where Beaux and the woman had been fucking and found the woman crumpled on the ground, holding her arm which seemed to have a nasty cut on it. In the dark he could see a dark fluid rushing down her arm and partially naked body.

The woman looked up at him, the familiar look that too many victims wore, confused.

"Rafe!" He heard Emily scream and stood quickly, searching the parking lot anxiously.

Grabbing his phone, he hurriedly pushed 911 and almost yelled at the dispatcher who answered.

Emily hurried toward him, but she wasn't coming from the direction of his car. Her words came through in pants and her hair was windblown around her face as if she'd just been running.

"God. Rafe. There are two of them."

Chapter Ten

ಬಾ

Too many thoughts rushed through Emily. It didn't dawn on her that they'd reached her apartment complex until he parked in front of her building next to her car and cut the engine.

"I know I'm right," she told him, still feeling adrenaline pumping through her veins as she fished for her keys in her backpack. "Beaux ran up the hill before she screamed. It was just like the first time."

"What do you mean by the first time?" Rafe asked when she unlocked her door.

"I guess I never told you," she said, watching as he entered her dark apartment, found the lights and then walked through every room before returning to face her in her living room.

He approached her like a predator, dark and dangerous, his hair curling around his face more so than usual after being out in the moist night air. Those green eyes penetrated right through her. His dark eyebrows made his eyes seem even darker. Watching her, not saying anything until he stopped right in front of her, she realized she'd held her breath and exhaled quickly.

"Maybe you should tell me now," he said quietly, his mood not readily obvious.

"You know I was parking in that lot every day during the first week of classes," she began, her mouth suddenly too dry.

Thoughts that he'd almost been charged with murder, that he had been a cop and wasn't one any longer, had her heart pounding way too hard in her chest. He looked more like a hardened criminal at the moment than an investigator who fought to uphold the law.

"Go on," he prompted, not touching her but standing so close that she couldn't breathe without inhaling his scent.

"When I went to my car one night…" She paused, sucking in a breath. "I heard a scream. I didn't do anything about it. I got in my car and left. The next day I saw there'd been a murder when I read it in the paper."

"And so you decided to turn into the private detective?" It was too hard to read him.

Rafe kept his expression so masked, she couldn't tell if he was outraged or simply curious to learn what she knew. And she really didn't know anything.

"I've always been fascinated by solving mysteries," she admitted.

He reached up, casually taking a strand of her hair and focusing on it while he twisted it around her finger. "Who did you tell about the first time?"

"No one." She chewed on her lip, watching him but he wasn't looking at her.

His expression seemed so intent on her hair, but there was something else, something deeper, she couldn't figure out what thoughts he might be having.

"And that night happened just like tonight?"

"Yes. I saw someone run up the hill. I remember thinking they ran up it so easily that they must be in incredible shape." She willed him to look at her and finally he did. "After I saw the person run up the hill, then I heard the scream."

She shuddered. Staring into those dark eyes, so deep with something carnal lingering, she forgot to breathe.

"Get your things," he told her, this time whispering. "And tomorrow, after a good night's sleep, we're going to go over every little detail you can think of."

She nodded, for some reason not in the mood to argue with him. She didn't want to be alone. They'd saved a woman's life tonight, although she'd probably be in the hospital for a while. The police would interrogate her, and hopefully she would shed some light on what happened. One thing Emily knew, and somehow it made sense. Beaux wasn't the murderer.

It fit. He didn't meet the profile she had in her mind of how a killer would be. Someone capable of murder would be more sinister, darker by nature—someone like Rafe.

A chill rushed through her as she grabbed a few things out of her bedroom and returned to his dark figure in her living room. He didn't say anything as he led her out the door.

Sometime during the night, Emily woke up in a strange bed. Darkness shrouded her and for a moment she simply stared wide-eyed at the ceiling, focusing on keeping her breath calm while she held the thick comforter to her chin like a shield.

Slowly it came back to her—Rafe bringing her to his house, giving her time in the bathroom and then snuggling her into bed. She must have fallen asleep quickly because she didn't remember anything after that.

What she did know was that right now, she was very much alone in the bed. Would he have slept on the couch, actually respecting her comment about not knowing him well enough?

There was no way she'd fall back asleep now. Taking a deep breath, she hurried out of bed and almost attacked the light switch. Standing there for a moment, wearing only her T-shirt, she took in the contents of his bedroom.

"And you told him you liked detective work," she mumbled, taking a deep sigh when light flooded the room.

She would make a lousy detective. Her own paranoia of the dark would keep her from seeing any clues during the night.

The hallway leading to the stairs wasn't quite as dark since light from the bedroom flooded through it. But the place was unsettling with how quiet it was. Making it to the bottom of the stairs, she searched the living room, not seeing Rafe on the couch or anywhere else for that matter.

"What time is it?" She searched for a clock, turning on lights as she moved through the place.

The digital clock on the microwave glowed in the dark kitchen. It was after two in the morning. She caught her own reflection in sliding glass doors at the end of the narrow kitchen and paused, backing away. Darkness lay beyond those windows, the unknown, in an unfamiliar neighborhood.

Turning back to the living room, she walked through it, staring at each painting on the wall, books and magazines shelved in a disorderly fashion on a tall wooden bookshelf, and then at a glass case housing a variety of rifles.

"What kind of man are you, Rafe?" she whispered, letting her gaze travel over the weapons.

Testing the latch, she was surprised to see that the glass case wasn't locked. The door opened silently, filling her senses with a unique mixture of smells. Rafe obviously took good care of these weapons. They all looked recently cleaned and very deadly.

Not daring to remove any of them, she ran her fingers over the smooth wood and hard metal of a rifle that looked like it was very old. Cold and dangerous, yet alluring and captivating, she ran her fingers along the length of the weapon.

Vague memories of going hunting with her uncles as a child came to mind, but they didn't use weapons like these. Normal hunting rifles obviously didn't appeal to Rafe. She noticed a silencer on the end of one of the guns and shivered. No. The type of weapon that obviously appealed to Rafe was one used for a much more serious type of attack.

Her heart raced while she studied the deadly weapons so beautifully displayed before her. A small cabinet was at the bottom of the glass display case and she knelt, opening it slowly. A small wooden box sat next to several jars of polish that he used on the guns. Lifting the box, she flipped the small latch and lifted the lid. A bright silver handgun, one you'd expect to see some top-notch spy use on TV, glistened in the light.

Standing up, she turned on the second lamp in the living room, giving herself more light, and then knelt again, studying the incredibly small but more dangerous-looking weapon than any of the rifles hanging in the case above.

Rafe had quite an impressive collection of weapons. She was no expert, but her guess was that none of these were used for hunting—hunting animals that is. These were the tools of his trade, of stalking and capturing criminals. And by the look of the amount of artillery displayed in front of her, he took his business very seriously.

Men back home collected street rods, motorcycles, and some of them had guns. But nothing like this. When she delicately lifted the small handgun out of its case, the hard metal cooled her palm. She ran her finger down the top of it, respecting how dangerous it was by keeping it flat in her palm, and her fingers away from the trigger.

Rafe liked danger, the hunt and more than likely the capture. Stroking the hard barrel, her insides swelled, captivated by something so beautiful, yet deadly.

A click sounded behind her, and she jumped, shrieking while she dropped the gun in her lap. Turning quickly, she stared at Rafe, his tall, broad frame filling his doorway. Bright green eyes glistened while his brown hair seemed to curl around his face more so than normal.

"Be careful. They're loaded." He shut the door behind him, locking it, then slowly strolled over to her. "Mind telling me why every light in my house is on?"

He stood over her, looking down with something akin to interest, possibly amusement showing in his face. Her neck strained, and she looked down at the loaded gun resting in her lap where she'd dropped it. He definitely didn't seem mad that she'd gone through his collection.

"I'm a little nervous in the dark," she told him, lifting the gun to put it back in its case. "Where did you go?"

"To the hospital." He squatted next to her, taking the gun from her hands, his powerful arms pinning her while he lifted the gun. "I wanted to be there when they interrogated the woman we saved earlier."

"Why didn't you take me with you?" She turned, which meant adjusting herself in his arms that he'd wrapped around her.

Suddenly she was inches from his face. His gaze dropped to her mouth.

"You have to go to work early in the morning," he explained, his tone calm and controlled. "If I'd told you I was going, you would have wanted to go with me."

"You're right."

He leaned over her further, putting the gun back into its case. "What do you know about weapons?" His voice barely a whisper.

"Not much," she admitted.

"Ever shot a gun?" he asked.

"A couple of times when I was a kid." She doubted an old rifle aimed at bottles on a fence at her uncle's farm counted. She'd never hit her target.

"Don't mess with things you don't understand," he told her.

She looked up at him. *I don't understand you.*

The case clicked closed but she didn't look down. His eyes were on hers and he ran a finger underneath her chin, tracing a path down to her collarbone.

"Maybe you could teach me," she whispered.

"Only if you agree to follow instruction."

Somehow she wasn't sure if he meant the guns.

"I guess that depends on how good of an instructor you are," she said, grinning into his handsome face.

Her heartbeat raced as he leaned into her, spreading his hand over her neck. "Behave, and you'll learn," he whispered, and then took her mouth.

Demanding and hot, his lips were moist when they opened over hers. His tongue warred with hers, consuming, taking everything she offered. It was all she could do to breathe.

His fingers wrapped around her neck, tipping her chin back to allow him deeper access to her mouth. She gasped when he nipped at her lower lip, the quick pinch of pain replaced with pleasure when he then sucked on the exact same spot.

Waves of desire surged through her, violent and strong.

"Rafe," she cried, reaching for him, suddenly feeling she would fall backwards if she didn't hold on.

He tightened his grip around her neck slightly. Opening her eyes, she stared into his smoldering gaze. She could breathe, but if he tightened his grip any further, she'd be gasping. Not a single muscle moved on his face when he quit kissing her and moved his head back a fraction of an inch, simply watching her.

Rafe had to be in control. She sensed that with the intensity of his gaze. If he didn't have complete power, she sensed he would fight until he gained it. Relaxing, she breathed slowly, making no attempt to move his hand but simply staring up at him.

Slowly, a smile crossed his face. Taming a man like him might be an impossible task. No wonder he'd told her he wouldn't make a good catch.

He let go of her neck and slid his hand down her front, brushing over her breasts, which ached for more attention. "You're soaked, Emily," he growled when his fingers moved under her shirt and between her legs.

"And I'm sure you're hard as a rock," she said mischievously, trying to turn so she could reach for his cock.

He stopped her. "This isn't about me," he said.

"Huh?" That made no sense.

But she didn't have time to dwell on his words. Hard and aggressively, at least two fingers impaled her soaked cunt.

"Oh God," she cried out, arching and bucking at the same time.

He pulled her shirt up, lifting it so that she almost fell backward, raising her arms so he could pull it over her head. Then she did lean back, falling to the floor while his fingers worked magic inside her.

"So tight and fucking perfect," he breathed above her.

Fogged with lust, she barely was able to form a thought. Once again she lay before him naked while he was fully clothed.

As quickly as he'd thrust his fingers inside her, he pulled them out. Lying on his living room floor, naked, she stared at him, barely able to catch her breath.

Still kneeling over her, he brought his fingers to his mouth, capturing her gaze as he sucked his fingers into his mouth. His eyes fluttered shut for the briefest of seconds, as if her taste was the best thing he'd ever had. Then his gaze focused on her, boring through her while he simply watched her. Waves of discomfort from him simply staring at her, naked and exposed, made her want to move, cover herself with her hands, anything.

"This isn't fair," she complained, moving her hand between her legs.

Instantly she brushed over her sensitive and soaked flesh and jerked from the movement. Instead of covering herself, now she simply wanted to continue where he left off.

"What isn't fair?" he asked, shifting his attention so that he watched her stroke her own pussy.

"You're still dressed."

"Then undress me," he told her, his green eyes deep pools of penetrating lust.

She moved so that she kneeled in front of him. He remained kneeling but was much taller than she was. Slowly, praying she could drive him to the same madness he'd brought her to, she began undoing the buttons on his shirt. Her fingers traced over his warm flesh, feeling hard, corded muscle twitch as she touched it.

Spreading his shirt open, she ran her hands over coarse dark hair that spread over his chest. Leaning into him, she kissed him and then moved to one of his nipples, lashing at it with her tongue.

Slowly moving to the other nipple, she did the same thing until the flat nipple puckered under her own method of retaliation.

Grabbing her hair, he yanked her head back then devoured her mouth. She ripped her mouth from his, gasping for breath, fighting not to give in to the incredibly primal acts he inflicted on her.

Placing her hand on his chest, she pushed until he straightened, looking down at her as if he'd pounce at any given moment.

"I'm not done," she whispered, knowing she pushed his level of self-control to the limit.

She reached for the top button of his jeans, the hair on his hard stomach torturing her skin. Rafe sucked in a breath when she stroked the length of his throbbing cock before slowly, very slowly, undoing his jeans.

"Stand," she ordered.

She didn't mean to meet his gaze, but when she did, she caught his raised eyebrow, the smoldering look in his eyes turning dark. Rafe didn't take orders well.

"If you don't, the jeans stay on," she said, managing a flirtatious smile even though the look he gave her made her tummy flutter.

Anticipation and the danger of the powerful man who made it clear he wanted her submission had her almost trembling. When he moved to his feet, standing over her, she remained on her knees, doubting her legs would hold her at the moment anyway. Tugging his jeans down his legs, his throbbing cock pounced to life, finally freed, and almost hit her in the face.

Rafe stepped out of his shoes and then his socks. He looked magnificent standing over her naked, powerful, and so much man she trembled with need.

Taking his cock in her hands, she pressed her lips to the swollen head, so soft, and sheathing muscle so hard it was like a rock.

"No, my dear," Rafe said, groaning when she brushed her lips over him.

She looked up, confused, tasting him on her lips and running her tongue over them.

Rafe bent over her, pushing her backward on his living room floor and then spreading her legs.

"I told you, this isn't about me."

Emily laughed, hiding her confusion. "If we do it right, it's about both of us."

"Not tonight," he said, his mouth already breathing against her pussy.

He kissed her gently and she closed her eyes, not having a damn clue what he meant but loving what he was doing to her so much that she didn't care.

She clawed at the carpet and her hand touched a small bag she hadn't noticed before. Turning her head, her gaze blurred as Rafe ran over her pussy with his tongue and then sucked her clit into his mouth.

She cried out, her hand clamping down on the bag. It took a moment for her to realize she'd grabbed something round and smooth inside the bag. Rafe continued applying very fine-tuned skills while pressure swarmed through her, growing with every stroke of his tongue.

"God," she cried, bucking against his face.

Rafe held her legs pinned, his fingers pressing into her flesh while he devoured her.

Every muscle in her body hardened, her back arching off the floor while she rode out the orgasm he'd brought her to way too quickly. Panting, she fought for enough air and for a moment was sure she'd float right off the ground. She was that lightheaded.

Her mind swirled. If this was what he meant by tonight not being about him, hell—she was all for it. It took her a minute to realize she gripped something in her hand. Turning her head, glancing at it through strands of hair that swept over her face, she frowned, fighting to regain control of her thoughts. Her pussy pulsed so fucking hard, all she wanted was for him to crawl over her and fuck the shit out of her.

"What's this?" she asked, barely able to catch her breath in order to speak.

"Take it out of the bag." He straightened, his hand replacing his mouth as he gently stroked her overly sensitive pussy.

She jumped against his touch and glanced up at him, barely able to lift the bag, let alone remove anything from it.

"Take it out," he repeated, watching her with an intent stare.

Her fingers didn't want to cooperate. She managed to remove a pale pink object, a dildo, except that it was soft—too damn soft to possibly be of any use. She bent it slightly between her fingers, realizing it was sturdier than it felt.

"I'd rather have you," she sighed, letting her hand with the toy in it drop to her side while she tried riding his hand.

He chuckled, reaching for her hand and lifting it with the toy and moving them between her legs.

"It's not for your pussy. It's for your ass."

She looked up at him wide-eyed, every muscle inside her tensing.

"Relax," he said soothingly, removing his hand from her pussy and stroking her stomach. "I promise. You'll love it."

"I've never…" she began.

"I know. That's why I got this for you. It will prepare you for me. I told you tonight is for you."

She watched with morbid curiosity when he took the toy from her hand and then spread her legs, running his fingers from her soaked pussy to the more sensitive flesh below. His focus on her was so serious, so focused, concentrating on what he did with the skill of a master. She was so damned soaked that his finger slid inside her ass and then glided around the edge of it with ease.

Again and again he ran his finger from her pussy to her ass, soaking her and lubricating her with her own cum. Every time he pressed his finger against her ass, and then entered it slowly, a pressure grew inside her, increasing every time he moved inside her.

And then something larger, harder, spread the tight hole open, stretching it, creating a burning that was accompanied by an intense pressure that made her want to buck into him. She licked her lips, opening her mouth to cry out but nothing was there. The sensations that rushed through her were too much. Barely able to catch her breath, she couldn't cry out, couldn't beg for more.

Damn. That's what she wanted too. More. Now. Harder. Deeper. He'd created a sensation that rushed through her, pushing her to the edge but not quite over. She teetered, fearing she would fall over the edge, exploding harder than she ever had before, and then not be there for him. It took more strength than she knew she had to try simply to hold on to reality and not come.

And then he entered her, raising her suddenly stiff legs, moving her while he drove his cock deep into her pussy.

"Fuck!" she screamed, clawing at the carpet and then reaching for him.

She could barely focus on the chuckle that tore through him, deep and dangerous.

Rafe increased the movement, the dildo stretching her ass while his cock impaled her pussy. A fire burned through her, intense and out of control. Nothing she could do would stop the explosion that tore through her.

Grabbing his shoulders, digging into his flesh, she howled, somewhere deep inside feeling foolish for getting off so hard with an act she would have refused to do if she'd been even remotely sane at the moment.

Rafe's strong body leaned over her, bringing her legs up so that they rested on his shoulders. She was forced to move her hands, grabbing her head as she turned it from side to side, unable to stop the orgasm that tore through her and threatened never to end.

Before it subsided, Rafe pulled out of her, leaving her breathless and burning for him to return to her. A strange sensation crept through her and she tried to look down, unable to focus. Suddenly the pressure built again and he looked down at her, those powerful green eyes deep smoldering pools, searing her with the same intensity that ripped through her body.

Once again he leaned over her, a pressure building through her, intense, clogging her ability to think and growing with every staggered breath. As she stared up at him, drowning in his gaze, his eyes brightened, intense satisfaction spreading across his face.

God. He was fucking her ass.

"Rafe," she gasped, the pressure building too quickly.

"God," he growled. "So fucking perfect."

It was too much. He moved in and out of her ass, gliding through the well-lubed, tight little hole, creating a sensation that threatened to consume her, take over. She'd go over the edge and feared she'd never return. Nothing had ever compared to this. With every plunge the force inside her built, fire and ice, smoldering and chilling her all at the same time.

"That's it, sweetheart. You're going to explode."

Forming words was too much to ask at the moment. She stared up at him, feeling his large cock ease in and out of her tight ass. She wanted more, needed more, harder—faster.

Opening her mouth, trying to tell him how she needed it, all that escaped her lips was a cry. Something broke inside her, gushing through her with more power than she'd ever experienced before. Her world spun around her. There was nothing to hold on to. Just when she knew she would pass out, die from the most intense orgasm she'd ever had in her life, Rafe grew inside her. A burning tore through her and at the same time he howled, a growl forming deep inside him and tearing through him until he threw his head back, letting more emotion escape from him with his guttural cry than she'd seen him display since she'd met him.

The fire inside her was instantly replaced with a soothing feeling. His hot cum soaked her ass, filling her, soothing the fire. Nothing she'd ever experienced in her life came close to what he'd just given her. An act so primal, so raw and intimate, she wasn't sure she'd ever be the same from the experience.

He lowered his mouth to hers, capturing her lip and nibbling on it while slowly gliding out of her.

"Emily," he growled into her mouth and then closed his mouth over hers.

Her arms seemed to weigh a ton when she slowly lifted them, pulling him to her, deepening the kiss.

Chapter Eleven

೩

Standing in the shadows, he watched through the dark window, his cock hardening when he heard their cries, their howls of pleasure. The asshole spilled everything he had into that slut. Reaching into his sweatpants, he stroked his hard cock, closing his eyes and briefly allowing his imagination to take over.

It wasn't fair that the creep got to enjoy Emily. Beaux would have his turn. He'd really make her howl. And now that he knew where she was—he grinned at his clever mind. That old fool thought he could outwit Beaux. Well, maybe it had been Mom who'd figured it out. But Beaux would have sooner or later.

Pretty damn clever of Rafe Healy telling him that he wasn't a cop.

Close enough. He was a fucking private investigator.

Beaux still grinned as he backed silently away from the window and moved through the shadows. The gated community was a farce, so easy to get in and out of. Following the investigator home from the hospital had been child's play. No thrill to it at all.

But watching him tear into that sweet thing he had at his house. Next time it would be his turn.

He sprinted across the parking lot, jumping at the gate and then lifting his body over it. There was too much energy rushing through him. Watching and not fucking had him all wired. He needed release. Needed it now.

Jumping into the passenger seat of his car, he didn't bother looking at Darlene. "Let's go home."

Her sulky attitude fucking pissed him off. He wanted pussy, ripe and wet. Now all he had was his wife. Mom would hear about this.

"What were you doing in there?" she asked after driving a few blocks.

Beaux looked over at her. Darlene's stringy brown hair clung to her head and then disappeared in the folds of her oversized sweatshirt. Mom made her dress like that. She was so damned skinny though, it really didn't matter what she put on, nothing would make her look any better.

"Watching this hot bitch get laid," he told her, lazily looking back at the street in front of him.

Darlene sighed. "I don't know why you just don't tell me the truth. We wouldn't fight so much if you just told me what you were really doing."

Beaux chuckled. "I just did."

They passed under a streetlight and for a moment the light accentuated her narrow cheek bones, making her pale blue eyes look hollow as she stared at him. He saw her face as a skeleton, strands of brown hair still stuck to her skull. Imagining her dead, no longer able to ask so many stupid questions, nag at him all the time, had him grinning.

"Why are you smiling?" she asked, that whining sound entering her voice.

"Nothing," he said.

He could picture her, lying in the ground, decaying, skin no longer on her bones. Staring at her face, once again in the darkness, it was easy to see the outline of her skull. And even with the baggy clothes she wore, visualizing her bony shoulders wasn't hard to do. Her thin arms, protruding hips and no ass. Just like a skeleton. Dead. No talking. No whining. No questions.

"Did you really watch people have sex?" she asked quietly.

"Yes."

"Why?"

"I wanted to."

"You're sick."

He hated that disgusted tone she took with him as much as her whining tone.

"Mom says I'm fine."

They pulled into the driveway and Darlene turned off the engine. "Your mom is sick too," she said under her breath.

"What?" He jumped out of the car. "What did you say?"

Darlene got out of the car but then moved backwards, that pathetic cowardly look spreading across her face.

"I didn't mean it," she said.

"I'm telling Mom." Maybe then Mom would see how Darlene really was.

"No!" Darlene threw herself at him, scratching his arm when she grabbed him. "I swear I didn't mean it."

Beaux jerked his arm, tearing himself free of her. She fell to the ground, crawling for a minute before trying to grab his legs.

"Tell Mom you didn't mean it." He reached the steps to the front door.

Darlene rushed him, trying her damnedest to get in the door before him. Such a baby. She always thought Mom would side with her over him. Mom loved him.

The two of them almost fought to get through the doorway at the same time.

"Wipe your feet," Mom said quietly.

Beaux froze, knowing when Mom spoke quietly she wasn't in a good mood. He hated it when Mom wasn't happy. Darlene quit moving as well, wiping her feet next to him on the floor mat just inside the door.

As usual, Mom sat in her rocking chair, facing the television with the remote in her lap. The television was muted, and Mom stared at the news, her expression strained. Beaux knew the sound of the TV bothered her. Sometimes he would go into the other room and watch the same show so that he could tell her what was said. Mom strained to hear the show that had no sound and didn't turn around to acknowledge them.

He wouldn't be able to tell on Darlene when Mom was paying such close attention to the news show.

"How are you, Mom?" Darlene moved around him, whispering her question and then kissing Mom gently on the cheek.

Beaux pursed his lips. Darlene shouldn't be able to do that. Mom approved so he couldn't stop her. But she was *his* Mom — not hers.

"I'm watching my show." Mom waved her hand in the air, sign enough to make Darlene cower away, quickly sitting on the floor a few feet from Mom.

One lamp lit the living room, casting shadows across the thin carpet. The firm couch and coffee table were the only furniture other than Mom's rocking chair. Darlene knew better than to sit on the couch. That was his spot.

Walking behind Mom, he relaxed onto the couch, taking his shoes off and then lying back. He watched the silent TV, wishing his mother would allow a bit of sound. It was impossible to figure out what they were talking about.

Finally, a commercial came on.

"What did you two do tonight?" Mom asked.

Darlene looked at him. She always looked worried when Mom asked questions. It surprised him sometimes that Mom didn't yell at her for it. Not that Mom really yelled. She didn't approve of it.

"We went to the hospital just like you asked," Beaux said, straightening the way she liked him to do when he spoke.

Mom stared at him for a moment. There was never any way to know what she was thinking. Since he was a kid that bugged him. Pale blue eyes watched him. Eyes that seemed so blank. Beaux knew better though. Mom was always thinking, figuring out everything.

Mom sighed. "Do I have to keep asking questions? What happened?"

"I'm sorry, Mom," he instantly blurted out.

"Sorry. Always sorry." She turned her attention to Darlene. "Do you have enough brains to tell me what happened?"

Darlene jumped, running her hands over her baggy sweatshirt that almost hung to her knees. "Yes, Mom."

"I can tell you. She doesn't know anything."

Mom turned and looked at him, slowly smiling. It made her cheeks wrinkle, although her eyes were still hollow and pale. Sometimes he thought her eyes would look the same if she were dead.

"You always try to make Mom happy," she said, using that soothing tone that made it so easy to relax.

He loved it when she spoke like that. Everything was okay when Mom used her soothing tone.

Beaux relaxed. "Darlene took her flowers just like you said to do. And then I discovered that one of the men in my classes is really a private investigator. Now I know where he lives."

Darlene gave him an odd look, but he ignored her. Mom would be pleased and he loved it when she praised him. She ran her thin hands over her jeans, keeping her gaze on him. Her lips almost pursed together and then relaxed. Her eyes — always the same — seemed to see right through him.

Slowly she stood, the remote falling to the floor without her noticing. Beaux's heart started pounding in his chest. From far away, in the deepest depths of his brain, the ringing echoed. He ignored it. Mom was about to give him attention. Nothing would interfere with that.

Mom was tiny just like Darlene, but he didn't picture her as a skeleton. Mom would never die. Never.

"Who is this detective?" Mom asked.

"Rafe Healy. He thinks he can outsmart me." Beaux smiled at Mom.

And she slapped him across the face. The sting of the slap made his eyes water but it wasn't half as bad as the humiliation rushing through him.

"I sent you to the hospital and you rush after some detective. What's wrong with you?"

"I did what you said, Mom." He held his hand to his cheek, staring past Mom to Darlene.

She picked at her tennis shoe, not looking at either one of them.

"Then what did the bitch say?" Mom asked.

"Darlene went into the room. You said to do it that way."

When Mom looked away from him, he sneered at Darlene. Mom would yell at her now. If Beaux could leave, just get up and walk out of the house, everything would be okay. Mom would join him. He wouldn't have to stare at Darlene. It might not be too late to find a piece of ass. That would make Mom happy. And he didn't want to have to fuck Darlene tonight.

"Please tell me you did what I told you to do." Mom sounded tired.

Beaux let his gaze travel over her back. Her short gray hair, cut close to her head, ended before her collar. Images popped into his head, his mother's backside, her shoulder blades pressing against her shirt. So small and thin yet a giant. She'd saved him. Kept him safe and protected him. Mom had told him she did it for him.

Closing his eyes wouldn't make the images go away. All the blood. Dripping, dark, rich and irony smelling.

Plunge! Plunge! Plunge!

He saw the knife slice through the air, soaked with blood and still shining when the light hit it.

"I didn't get to hear anything, Mom. There were men in there but they stopped talking when I entered." Darlene was talking way too fast. "She had bandages on her and machines beeped around her. But she looked okay. She'll be all right."

Darlene smiled, the stupid bitch. She didn't understand anything.

"Obviously you two can't pull off a simple job." Mom was shaking her head, slowly reclining back into her rocking chair. "Where is my remote?"

Beaux reached for it at the same time that Darlene knelt across the floor, also trying to pick it up. Beaux snatched it before she could get it.

"Here it is, Mom," he said, offering it to her.

"Put it on my lap," she ordered.

Beaux gently placed the small black remote on her lap. Mom grabbed his hand, keeping it on her lap.

"Darlene. Go to your room." She didn't look at his wife.

Beaux smiled. All of Mom's attention was on him.

Darlene almost ran from the room. That was fine with him. Life was better when he was alone with Mom.

"Mom will make everything better."

"Yes. I know." He relaxed his hand when Mom moved it to her button on her jeans.

When she stood again, he helped her undress, not paying attention to her old and wrinkled body. Mom would never die. Ever since that terrible day, the day that Father died, Mom promised him she would always make everything all right.

The ringing started in his head again when he put his head between his Mom's legs, doing her just the way she liked. Her soft groans were quickly drowned out as the ringing increased. Closing his eyes, his movements automatic as he made Mom happy, the ringing escalated.

Beaux balled his hands into fists, pressing them against the floor as he leaned forward on his hands and knees. The voices returned. He hated the voices. If he didn't please Mom she would get mad. Desperately trying to satisfy her the way she'd instructed so many years ago, when he'd still been a boy, he fought the voices that consumed him, painfully screaming through his head.

What have you done?

The question echoed through his head, reverberating off his skull. The painful question, screeched with its hissing sound, always made him jump.

What have you done?

The voices were strong, more so than usual. They were getting worse but there was nothing he could do about it. He wouldn't be able to fuck them away tonight. Jacking off only suppressed them for a few minutes, sometimes not that long.

Mom caressed his shoulder. "It's okay, my little boy. You know Mom won't let anyone hurt you."

He loved the way she soothed him with her words, always there to take care of him. But the voices, still echoing, repeating the same question over and over again, made it hard to hear her. He hated the voices. They wouldn't go away. But there was no way to kill a voice, not without a body. And the bodies were long gone.

What have you done?

You did this. Not me.

You killed her. You butchered her to death. My God. The blood.

The laughter was as bad as the voices. Not happy laughter, but mad laughter. Beaux hated mad laughter. Every muscle in his body hardened. Mom would be mad. Focus on Mom. Ignore the voices. Don't listen to them. Make Mom happy.

Anyone you fuck I will kill!

The sentence echoed, bouncing through his head, floating through his bloodstream, repeating itself over and over again.

"Mom," he cried, unable to continue giving her what she wanted. "Make them stop, Mom."

Mom grabbed his head, her cold fingers pressing against his brain. "You're being a bad boy, Beaux," she whispered.

Beaux squeezed his eyes shut. The pain in his head made it impossible to move. The voices overlapped each other now, everyone talking at once.

The screaming.

The blood.

The shiny knife streaked with rich, dark blood, dripping, dripping everywhere.

What have you done?

You killed her.

Anyone you fuck I will kill!

Everything at once.

The words on top of each other.

Screaming and yelling.

Death and murder.

"No!" Beaux forced himself backward, falling over his legs.

He wouldn't hurt Mom. The voices wouldn't stop. He grabbed his head, rolling on the floor. Fuck.

"I need to fuck," he whimpered.

"It's okay, my little boy." Mom bent over him, naked, not looking like the old woman anymore but the young lady who'd killed Dad. "I will take care of everything. I always do, don't I?"

"Yes," he cried, his fingers digging into his hair, grabbing his skull, pressing so hard but not able to get the voices out.

Mom leaned over him, speaking so quietly it was hard to hear her over the voices. "Go fuck Darlene. Beaux. Fuck

Darlene. Do as you're instructed. As I've always instructed you. Gain your pleasure and pull out before you come. Mom will take care of you."

Beaux opened his eyes. Mom was a blur. Everything was a blur.

"You will kill her?" he asked.

"Pull out before you come so there are no babies and I will kill anyone you fuck." She smiled.

The voices stopped.

Beaux sat up, his vision clearing and his head finally quiet.

"You will kill Darlene?" He loved Mom.

"Go fuck her. Mom will take care of you."

Chapter Twelve

❧

"It was all just too bizarre," Mary said, hugging herself and looking from one police officer to the next. She spotted Emily walking across the street toward the front of the bar and reached for her. "I'm so glad you're here."

Emily took in Mary's pale face, the way her hand shook, and the police and ambulances parked along the side of the street. *Not again,* she thought to herself.

"What happened?" Emily asked, already dreading the answer.

"Miss. We'd like to ask you a few more questions." The young officer's expression was serious, although his tone gentled as he focused on Mary. "Would you mind coming to the patrol car with me?"

"Emily, come with me." Mary clung to her for dear life.

Emily's heart went out to her. So young, and away from home for the first time in her life, Emily knew that Mary looked to her like an older sister. She wouldn't say like a mom. She wasn't that damn old.

The officer nodded that it would be okay. Mary leaned against Emily as they walked to the car. Brisk air wrapped around her, the fall breeze sending dead leaves scampering around their feet.

The heated patrol car warmed her instantly when she entered the backseat on the opposite side of Mary. Shutting the car door, she saw Rafe's Firebird pull up across the street. They were supposed to meet here. She watched him, growing accustomed to his facial expressions over the past week that she'd been staying at his town home. He ran his hand through his thick brown hair and stopped to talk to the officer standing outside.

"Mary Ziegler, is it?" the officer in the front seat asked, appearing to be looking at her driver's license.

"Yes." Mary reached for Emily's hand and squeezed it.

Emily had no idea what was going on other than Mary was very upset about something. Her thoughts drifted to the worst though.

The officer straightened a form on a metal clipboard and snapped a pen open. "Go ahead and tell me what you saw."

Mary squeezed her eyes shut. "Way too much blood," she began and then took a deep breath, shuddering uncontrollably. "I went out back to throw trash in the dumpster. She was next to the dumpster, naked and so red with blood."

Mary's free hand went to her mouth and Emily instinctively pulled her into her arms. The younger girl started crying.

"It was so awful. I've never seen anything like it," she said.

The officer turned around, looking sympathetic. "I'm sorry to do this to you. But if you can tell me if you saw anyone else. Was there anyone else in the alley?"

Mary shook her head, cuddling into Emily like a child. "Is it okay if I call my parents?"

Emily got out of the squad car a few minutes later, leaving Mary on the phone talking to her mother. More than likely Mary would be going home. This was too traumatic for her to deal with by herself. It was a damned shame. A young girl, simply working through her education, scarred by such a terrible crime.

Walking around to the back of the bar, she managed to move around yellow tape without anyone stopping her. It wasn't until she saw the naked body lying on the ground, covered in blood, that she almost gagged. The smell of blood was too thick in the air. But that wasn't what made her sick to her stomach. It should have. But for some reason, watching while an officer removed a large dildo from the woman and secured it in a ziplock bag, she felt her stomach turn.

Turning from the scene, needing fresh air, she hurried to the front of the bar. Students had gathered, curious and whispering among themselves, but she ignored them. No one noticed as she hurried across the street. Leaning against Rafe's Firebird, she held her stomach—that damn dildo still a clear image in her head.

She sensed him behind her before turning. Strong hands ran down her arms, controlling, possessive, demanding. Turning slowly, she met Rafe's brooding stare.

"Where have you been?" That was Rafe.

Nothing but the truth satisfied his protective nature, a trait that had its appeal. Her insides tightened as she continued to look at him. No matter the atrocity that she'd just seen, the heat of his gaze made her heart flutter.

Forcing her gaze away, looking past him at the bar, she sucked in a breath. Unfortunately, she inhaled Rafe's scent—leather, cologne and something unique to him. Her pussy swelled and she forced herself to ignore the carnal need that he seemed to bring out in her.

"I was in the squad car with Mary when you showed up. She wanted me there." Emily licked her dry lips.

Frustration surged through her that the killer had struck again. Along with that, Rafe stood so close to her, his gaze piercing right through her to the spot that seemed to send all of her nerve endings into a raging uproar. It was damned hard to think straight.

"So she was the witness they mentioned having, the young girl who works here and with you at The College Pub?" He stroked the side of her cheek, seeming to sense her turmoil but only making it worse with his touch.

Emily nodded, the roughness of his fingers making her insides quicken.

"I need to talk to a few people still," he told her, pulling his keys out of his pocket and then reaching around her to unlock his car. "You've got your cell phone on you, right? Stay in the car and keep it locked. Call me if anyone bothers you."

Images of the dead woman, covered in blood, her life ripped out of her, made her sick to her stomach.

"Okay," she said, although the last thing she wanted to do was sit alone in his car.

He seemed satisfied that she'd obey him and left her once he was assured both doors were locked. Emily sat staring at the dark dash, alone in the car, her mind going over the details she knew of the murders. It would be so easy to let the heavy scent of Rafe that saturated through everything inside the car take over. Drowning in it right now would ease her thoughts. He would be back soon and take her away from here, to his place, more than likely to hours of hot and passionate sex.

Her body tingled as she allowed her thoughts to drift to Rafe. Glancing through the windshield, over toward the bar, more than a handful of officers and reporters stood around, anxiously working while medics rolled a body toward the ambulance. Rafe stood with his back to her, talking to the officer she'd seen before. The other officers seemed to linger around Rafe as well. He had an aura about him. Even in his casual attire, his hair a bit longer than a professional would wear it, there was something about him that demanded the attention of those around him.

While she watched him, another officer approached, carrying a bag that more than likely held evidence in it from the murder. In spite of how her body warmed staring at Rafe, an image of the officer removing the dildo from the dead woman distracted her thoughts.

Then another thought hit her. The old woman who'd been in the alley had a large purse filled with dildos that looked just like the one that the officer had pulled from the corpse. Suddenly all the warmth that had seeped through Emily dissipated, a chill rushing through her. It had been the damnedest thing that an old woman would have so many identical dildos on her.

Another thought hit her, too bizarre to be counted, yet it wouldn't go away. The woman who'd been stabbed the other night hadn't been stabbed by Beaux. Someone else had stepped in, attacking her after Beaux had fucked her. They'd both seen Beaux take off running. Although the woman hadn't been much help when interrogated, saying she'd had her back to her assailant, it had been obvious that it wasn't Beaux.

But an old woman?

Emily shook her head. No way could an old woman manage to stab another person to death. It didn't take physical strength to push a knife through flesh. But it did take a hell of a lot of hatred. What kind of sick person would go around killing women and stuffing dildos in them right after the women had sex?

And all of the women seemed to be having sex with Beaux.

The murderer was killing women right after he'd slept with them. And not just killing them, stabbing them repeatedly, humiliating them—like the murderer was outraged.

A wife would be outraged if her husband was out fucking other women.

Emily sat up straight. A wife.

The strange lady who drank ice coffee at The College Pub, Darlene Robinson, was Beaux's wife. Emily hadn't seen her in there all week. Maybe another visit to her house would be in order. If only she could think of a good reason to pay a call.

* * * * *

Carlos wasn't good company the next morning. Although he grumbled that he understood why Mary quit with no notice, wrapping up her affairs and leaving town less than twenty-four hours after stumbling upon a gruesome murder, he didn't like it. Emily assured him she'd worked more than one station before in much busier restaurants, but that didn't seem to appease Carlos.

Avoiding him, doing her work, kept her busy through her entire shift. She'd barely taken a second to breathe when it was time to go.

"I can only find more help so fast," Carlos said with a shrug when Emily untied her apron after her shift.

"Don't worry about it, Carlos." She tried to sound reassuring. "I'll see you tomorrow."

She was worn out and had worked well past her shift helping the other women get restocked so they wouldn't start their shift with empty napkin holders and salt and pepper shakers. And after work she'd told Rafe she would head up to the library to do some research, but there was something she needed to do first.

Pulling her cell phone out as she hurried to her car, she punched in the numbers for Rafe's phone. His baritone sounded in her ear as it went to voice mail. Damn.

Climbing into her car, she stared for a moment at passing traffic on the street, her phone in hand. Rafe craved solving this case on his own. More than anything she wanted that for him. Thoughts of Beaux's wife, of how unstable she was—it all made sense. His infidelity pushed her over the edge. To the point of murder.

Emily pushed the buttons on her cell again. "Come on, answer," she grumbled.

Again Rafe's phone went to voice mail.

Where the hell was he?

"If I didn't answer, you'd throw a fit." She glared at her phone before tossing it on the passenger seat.

"I can't just go over there by myself." She chewed her lip, scowling at the street outside her car. "But if his wife didn't suspect the reason for my visit..." Nerves twisted in her stomach painfully. Biting down on her lip too hard, she touched herself with her fingers and frowned at her phone.

Maybe he was at his house and just not answering for some reason. Within less than ten minutes she parked in front of his town house, his Firebird nowhere in sight.

"You better answer," she told her phone, punching the number for Rafe.

Voice mail.

"Damn it."

Somehow she was going to talk to Beaux's wife again. Maybe alone would be better. Darlene might have been intimidated by Rafe's presence. Fear sent chills down her spine. Approaching someone capable of murdering many women without backup was plain stupid.

Emily valued her life.

Storming toward his front door, irritation irked her. She and Rafe needed to have a long talk. If she didn't answer her phone for him, he'd explode right through the ceiling. He'd damn well give her the same consideration.

Unlocking the door with the key he'd given her, she entered the dimly lit living room. Rafe's scent lingered heavily in the air. Everywhere she looked, everything she touched, had Rafe's mark on it. Like entering the den of a powerful predator, her nerves didn't settle when she found the phonebook.

Thumbing through it quickly, she traced her finger down the page until she found the number she needed.

"Hi. Yes. I'd like to speak with Officer Tangari," she said, remembering the cop who'd seemed to know Rafe well, having advised her to be careful around him.

"I can send you over to his voice mail," the indifferent-sounding dispatcher told her.

So much for taking that advice.

She was getting damned tired of voice mail. Hanging up before the recorded message ended, she glared at her surroundings.

She gave herself a harsh reprimand when she'd accepted how she would do things. "If you do anything other than see if she's free for lunch, Rafe won't have to kick your ass." She'd kick her own ass.

Her stomach twisted in knots, her palms suddenly too damp against the steering wheel. Her heart pounded so hard in her chest as though it would explode.

All she would do was drive to Beaux and Darlene's house. Practicing her friendly, not a care in the world smile, she rehearsed what she'd say. Claim that she was new in town, had no friends and missed talking to her at The College Pub. Then ask her to lunch.

Hopefully somehow she could gather some proof, something strong enough that it would warrant investigation that would support her theory. Because at the moment, Emily was willing to bet that Darlene quite possibly was the murderer.

It made sense. Beaux was her husband and a slut. He slept with any woman he could get his hands on. Although Emily couldn't see that leading to murder, she'd be the first to admit that Darlene wasn't stable. Hell, she was plain weird. Living with an unfaithful husband may have made her that way. Emily would leave that up to the psychiatrists to determine.

All she was going to do right now was find some sort of proof that Darlene killed those women. Then she'd tell Rafe what she found out, deal with his wrath and let him solve the crime.

If only he'd answer his damn phone.

Maybe it would be smarter to put this off until she'd reached him. One more time she tried his phone. No answer. Where in the hell was he?

Thoughts distracted her and before she realized it, she drove past Beaux Robinson's house. Well, she'd come this far. Hopefully there was no harm in simply talking to the woman. It wasn't like she was trying to go after her husband. After circling the block, doing her best to see the house at all angles, she parked one street over and then locked her car.

"It's even daylight," she whispered to herself.

There was nothing to be afraid of when it was light out.

Of course, a good detective would prowl through a neighborhood at night. Emily had watched more than enough television to know that all the really terrible crimes were solved after dark. Well, she would just have to make an exception to that rule.

No matter that the sun warmed her back while a brisk breeze lifted her hair, no one seemed to pay any attention to her as she walked down the gravel alley that split the block in half. She stopped when she reached the backyard of the small house where Beaux and Darlene Robinson lived.

Many of the houses had small single car garages along the alley, with off alley parking that led into their backyard. The Robinson house didn't have a garage. A simple backyard, neatly mowed with no flowers adorning it, or anything giving indication they spent much time outside.

Tall, wooden, privacy fences ran along the property line on either side of their one-story home, offering a small amount of seclusion. One tall plastic trashcan sat outside the backdoor with a lid on it. Emily chewed her lower lip, staring at the simple layout of the home. Not one damn thing made the place stick out. Staring at the home, icy chills rushed over her skin, giving her goose bumps.

She'd come this far. Instinctively running her fingers over her cell phone that she'd attached to the waist of her jeans, she sucked in a breath. Walking along the edge of the property, she glanced toward the driveway out front. Beaux's car wasn't parked in the drive. Emily let out a breath. She could only hope that Darlene was here.

Moving toward the house, she bit her lower lip, keeping an eye on the windows. Either there were no curtains or they were pulled back. She saw easily into a kitchen as she moved alongside the house. She squinted to see better as daylight put a glare on the glass. There was no movement inside the house. It would be just her luck to get the nerve to come this far and then no one be here.

When she reached the corner of the back of the house, her heart hurt from pounding so hard. She needed to get a grip on herself. Neighbors wouldn't see her with the privacy fences guarding her actions. Even if she was spotted, it wasn't so odd for a visitor to approach from the back of the house. No one would have reason to question her actions. Consoling herself didn't seem to do a bit of good. A tiny twig snapped when she stepped on it, and Emily jumped.

She was one hell of a detective—scared of the dark and the smallest sound during the day. Shaking her head, she told herself once again that no one would find her actions the least bit odd.

There were more branches and dried leaves alongside the house and even though she did her damnedest to move quietly, it seemed she stepped on every twig and leaf. Walking to the first window on the side of the house, she realized quickly that blinds were closed over it inside. But then she just stared at the windowpane for a moment. It seemed hundreds of flies buzzed against the inside of the glass.

Emily stared in horror at the sight, her stomach quickly turning. Why in the hell would there be so many flies inside the house? Bile rose in her throat as she watched the insects crawl against the blinds, buzzing and jumping over each other, as if trapped between the blinds and the glass.

"What the hell?" she whispered, instinctively backing away from the grotesque sight.

Flies congregated around trash and…dead things. For a moment the awful taste wouldn't leave her mouth. She thought for sure she would puke, her imagination running rampant as thoughts of why so many flies could be in that room plagued her.

She couldn't take her attention from the window as she reached for her phone. Whatever was in that room, it was wrong and disgusting. She just knew it. There were too many flies. Her fingers shook and her hands were damp with nervous sweat as she punched the numbers to call Rafe.

This time she'd leave a message. "Rafe, I'm at Beaux's house," she began. "Where are you?"

Taking a step backward, her foot hit something hard and she lost her balance. Something clamped around her ankle, biting into her, sending pain rushing through her body so fast and hard that she bit her lip.

"Oww!" she screamed, tripping when she couldn't move her foot and sending her phone sprawling across the yard.

Her hands hit the ground hard and she turned, looking at her foot when she couldn't move it. Some kind of animal trap, metal and heavy and chained to a corkscrew buried in the ground, wrapped around her ankle. She'd seen things like this on TV but never in person. Two metal clamps had closed around her ankle. It was a bear trap or something, although she imagined if she were a bear, she'd be able to break free.

The metal dug into her skin, her short ankle socks and tennis shoes not enough to keep it from her flesh. The metal was cold, and she plopped on her bottom, reaching for it but unable to move it to free her foot. Panic swept through her and she looked around her wildly.

"You've sprung a trap," a crackly voice said.

Emily twisted her body toward the front of the house and stared into the cold gaze of the old woman she'd seen in the alley.

"Help me, please," Emily pleaded.

The old woman turned, disappearing around the front of the house. Emily twisted around on the ground, crumpled leaves sticking to her. Attempting to stand, she couldn't see over the privacy fence into the neighbor's yard. She searched the ground, frantically looking for her phone. It lay several feet from her, half buried in leaves. She couldn't tell if the connection to Rafe's phone was still on or not.

"Rafe. I need help," she cried out, unsure if her plea would record on his voice mail or not.

No one was anywhere around her. Unable to see over the fence or around either the front or back of the house, Emily cried out, knowing someone had to hear her in this residential neighborhood. There had to be people nearby somewhere.

"Help! Anyone?" she yelled.

The eerie sensation that not another soul existed in this entire block other than her and the old woman crept through her.

Footsteps sounded behind her and she turned, almost falling again when the trap kept her foot from turning with her.

"Normal people knock on the front door." The old woman gave her an odd look.

Emily glowered at her. "Normal people don't have traps dug into their yard."

The old woman chuckled. "Seems to have served its purpose nicely."

Icy chills rushed through Emily. The woman's tone was sinister. Watching her warily, the woman's cold gaze wasn't half as disturbing as her appearance. Very short gray hair barely covered her head, allowing Emily to see the natural shape of her head, down to the curves of her skull. The woman was thin, almost gaunt, her skin wrinkled. She was small-boned, but not enough muscle and fat covered her body.

With a second glance, Emily realized what really struck her as eerie was how the woman dressed. She wore tight blue jeans, her protruding hipbones visible through the fabric. Bright pink tennis shoes matched a tight-fitting pink sweater that had tiny teddy bears over one small breast. Pale blue eye shadow made her eyelids appear to sink around her almost clear blue eyes. Blotches of blush did nothing to hide how sunken her cheeks were. And the worse part, Emily realized, fighting not to stare too hard, was the bright shiny pink lip-gloss spread over where her lips should be.

The woman must have sensed her staring because she grinned, showing off brown teeth, at least the teeth that were there. There were gaps appearing dark and adding to her eerie appearance.

For such a tiny older woman, the lady staring at her had such an incredibly odd appearance it made her look dangerous. Trepidation soaked through Emily. She watched the old woman hold a large metal key and then look down at the trap that painfully squeezed into Emily's ankle.

At that moment someone pulled into the driveway, and the old woman turned and then walked away from Emily without a word.

"Hey," Emily cried after her, looking down at her trapped ankle. "You aren't going to leave me here, are you?"

It wouldn't be Rafe. He wouldn't pull into the driveway. Turning, she looked longingly at her phone, out of reach, lying in the grass and damp leaves. As she stared at it, it lit up and in the next second started ringing.

Holy shit! Now what!

Going down on her knees, she stretched her body, lying on the ground, getting her clothes messed up as she struggled to reach her phone.

"Oh hell," the older woman said from behind her. "Get that phone."

Someone else stepped over her, the first thing Emily seeing was large shoes and pant legs. The phone was snagged off the ground and quit ringing right after that. Then large hands gripped her, picking her up quickly.

"Ouch!" she howled when she was stretched further than the trap would allow her ankle to go.

"Don't dismember her, you fool," the older woman scolded and knelt down in front of Emily with a large metal key in her hand.

Metal clanked and suddenly coldness surrounded her ankle. Emily looked down to see the old woman's hand rubbing her ankle and foot. She was free. Twisting out of the arms that held her, ignoring the stab of pain in her ankle, she gawked at Beaux Robinson who gave her an awkward smile.

"What are you doing here?" he asked.

"I…um…"

"Take her inside." The older woman straightened, her pale blue eyes looking far from pleased when she stared at Emily.

"I don't need to go inside," she said quickly. Although that was the reason she'd come here, wasn't it?

"Emily," Beaux said, sounding reprimanding. It was a tone she hadn't heard out of him before. "Mom said to go inside."

His mother? Emily frowned. "I did want to speak with Darlene."

They'd rushed her to the front of the house and inside the house without a word. Emily realized Beaux still had her phone in his hand, and reached for it. He held it up, looking at it as if he wasn't sure how it had gotten in his hand.

She tried taking it from his hand, managing to get her hand on it, when Beaux clamped down on her phone and her hand.

"You finally came to see me," he said, looking down at her. "I knew you'd realize I'd be better than that old detective you were fucking."

"What?" the older woman almost shouted. "Detective?"

"Remember the man I told you about, Mom?" Beaux sounded like a small boy when he talked to his mother.

Emily yanked her hand from Beaux, but he grabbed her wrist, grinning down at her as if she were a prize he refused to let go of. Fear jerked through her, hardening her muscles and making it hard to breathe.

"Let go of me," she said quietly.

"Beaux. You foolish child." The older woman shook her head, her tone hushed and reprimanding.

Something about her gaze sent icy chills running down Emily's back.

"Where is Darlene?" Emily asked, already sensing these two both had a few screws loose. But with Beaux refusing to keep his hands off her, and apparently indifferent that his own mother see him fondling her, she didn't wonder why the wife might have completely lost it and started murdering people.

Beaux's mother shrugged. "Take her to see Darlene."

"Okay, Mom." Beaux spoke quietly, almost reverently. "You always know best."

"Of course I do. You can have her in there."

Emily looked at the older woman. What had she just said?

"Have who in where?" She didn't like this.

Beaux didn't answer her, and neither did his mother. He started dragging her through the living room, leading her through the house. The direction they were heading was toward the room where all the flies were.

Emily's stomach clenched then swelled to her throat. Panic rushed through her so quickly that she stumbled.

"Where are we going?" she mumbled, suddenly digging in her heels.

Beaux didn't look at her but past her, at his mother. "She's fighting me, Mom."

"You better hurry up. Do as I say now." Her tone was shrill, suddenly so aggressive and assertive that Emily jumped.

Again Beaux seemed to pay little attention to her but dragged her to a hallway. His large hand wrapped around her wrist, making her sweat under his touch. Her hand slid in his, twisting, her skin stretching underneath his. Her cell phone stopped her hand from completely sliding out of his. She tried reaching for it with her other hand.

Before she could switch her phone to her other hand, it vibrated and then rang. The shrill sound made her jump.

Beaux reached for a door. Everything inside her began to spin. Flies. Flies on the window. They were everywhere. Her stomach churned.

"No. Don't."

She was too late.

Beaux opened the door. Dragging her into the dark room, flies flew around them. Hordes of them. Everywhere. Emily ducked instinctively, suddenly fighting him with everything she had.

She wasn't sure what made her look up. Maybe it was Beaux turning on the light. But she did. She looked up. And that's when she saw her. Lying on the bed, a look of horror still plastered on her gray face, Darlene lay naked and very, very dead.

"Oh God," Emily cried out, and then shut her mouth quickly as she fanned her face with her free hand.

Flies swarmed around her.

Somehow she got away from Beaux. Backing out of the room, she darted toward the door, only to run into his mother. The woman was a hell of a lot stronger than Emily would have guessed.

Images of Darlene, flies covering the black holes where her eyes would have been, her mouth open, a scream probably escaping from her when she died, had flies crawling in and around her lips. And the blood. Dried and putrid.

Emily gagged, coughing, pushing against Beaux's mom as she struggled to get past her.

"I don't like it in there, Mom." The calm tone Beaux used turned her blood to ice.

Flies swarmed through the house along with a smell so nauseating that Emily couldn't breathe without gagging.

It took her a minute to realize her phone was ringing again. She shook so hard she couldn't push the button to answer it. Fumbling, she managed to accept the call.

Beaux's mother grabbed the phone from her and threw it across the room.

"You're sick," she screamed. "God. Get me out of here."

"I don't like the way it rings." She spoke too calmly after such an intense act.

Everything was like a terrible nightmare. Words didn't match actions. Darlene lay on the bed dead, decaying without either one of them seeming to care. Flies buzzed around them and neither of them swatted at them.

"You said I could fuck her." Beaux whined like a baby.

"Shut up. Now we have to leave." Beaux's mother pushed away from Emily and turned toward the door.

Emily shoved the woman to the ground and raced toward the door. Why the hell did she park her car so far away from this house?

Chapter Thirteen

ॐ

Rafe almost threw his cell phone against the dash of his car. Fire burned through his veins. Every muscle inside him tensed, anger raging through him with a vengeance so hard he couldn't see straight.

"Answer your fucking phone," he growled, holding the phone so hard in his hand he almost crushed it.

Surprise rushed through him when Emily's phone quit ringing. "Emily," he yelled.

No one answered.

But he heard something. Listening intently, he heard voices. No matter how hard he concentrated, he couldn't make out the words. A crashing sound exploded against his eardrum. He didn't dare pull the phone from his ear, enduring the pain.

Then someone screamed. "You're sick," he thought he heard Emily say.

Rafe pounded his dash with his fist. There was only one explanation. For whatever reasons, Emily had sought out Beaux. And now she was in trouble.

Tossing his cell phone onto the passenger seat, he peeled away from the curb, pushing the speed limit as he hurried over to Beaux's home. There was no car in the drive when he pulled up out front of the nondescript-looking home.

Rafe grabbed his phone and patted the gun attached to his belt as he hurried up to the front door of the house. Several quick pounds on the front door didn't bring anyone running. He walked around the house and stopped before reaching the backyard.

"What the fuck?" He looked down at an older-model bear trap, which had tripped and unlocked.

No one had bothered to reset it. But it was hooked to a chain and corkscrew that was twisted deep into the ground.

"Son of a bitch," he cursed, noticing how it had been dragged around the small area of grass surrounding it, causing scrapes in the ground around it.

Rafe straightened slowly, everything around him feeling wrong. He had nothing to put his finger on, but he'd find it. He studied the length of the privacy fence that ran the property length and then looked over along the side of the house.

"Oh shit." He stared at the window, hundreds of flies hovering between the glass pane and blinds that hid whatever was inside.

Grabbing his cell phone off his belt, he marched around to the back of the house. He saw no one, not even a neighbor. Another privacy fence ran along the other side of the house as well.

"Tangari," Rafe said into the phone when the officer answered. "You might want to get over to 220 Maple Street."

"What's going on?" Tangari asked.

Rafe didn't see any reason to knock. He'd pounded on the front door, traipsed around the side of the house. They'd had plenty of time to acknowledge him.

Jumping up, he kicked the back door with all of his might. It flew open, slamming against the wall in the kitchen.

"I just kicked the door to the house in," Rafe said calmly, feeling incredible satisfaction from the act.

"What?" Tangari screamed. "Healy! If you do anything stupid…"

"Get your ass over here," Rafe interrupted. "You can book me when you get here, if you want."

180

He ignored the cursing that spewed into his ear and focused on the quiet kitchen. "Anyone home?" he hollered, already sensing he was very much alone in the house.

"Whose house is it? That address rings a bell." Tangari was huffing into the phone, more than likely racing through the building to his car.

"Beaux Robinson's," Rafe told him, walking through the kitchen into a family room, living area.

Everything appeared in order, but something didn't sit right. First of all, the house was full of fucking flies. Yet, he saw no trash, no food lying around. Curtains were closed. There wasn't a single picture hanging on a wall anywhere. The living room was sparsely furnished, a couch, rocking chair and TV in the corner.

He walked to the middle of the room, swatting at flies and then covering his nose.

"It fucking stinks in here," he said into his phone. "You still there?"

Rafe heard a car start through the phone. "On my way now. Why are you there?"

Quickly, he told Tangari that Emily hadn't been where they'd arranged to meet. "And it's not like her to not answer her phone. She always has it on and usually has it on her."

"So you suspect foul play?" Tangari was driving now.

"Well, we didn't get in a fight, if that's what you're wondering."

Rafe didn't want to touch anything, not even the lights. He walked across the room, aware that the stench was getting stronger. There were two objects on the floor. One of them was a remote.

"Fuck," he explained when he reached the second object. "I just found Emily's cell phone. Goddamn it."

"Calm down, Healy. We'll find her."

But would they find her in time? And what the hell was that fucking smell?

Not able to stand it any longer, he walked over and opened the front door, then propped open the screen door, allowing some of the flies to escape. They seemed to be everywhere.

Following the flies out front, he gasped for fresh air, looking up and down the street. If that bastard laid a hand on Emily, he would personally see to his execution.

Rafe met the squad car at the curb when Tangari pulled up behind Rafe's Firebird. Another squad car approached from the other end of the block, slowing and parking on the opposite side of the street.

"Dear God. Who died in here?" Tangari asked when Rafe led the way back into the empty house. "You realize it's going to be my ass if we don't find anything. It will be a few hours before I secure a search warrant."

"Then don't touch anything." Rafe hated the fucking red tape cops had to leap through just to solve a crime. "But here is Emily's cell phone. It was lying right over there."

He pointed to the corner of the room. "And I know she answered it when I called her. Somehow it got thrown across the room. That was about thirty minutes ago."

Tangari took the phone and pressed buttons on it. "You're right. It shows she took a call from you around thirty-four minutes ago."

Fire burned through Rafe. There was no way to reach Emily, make contact with her, without her phone. His mind raced to figure out where Beaux would have taken her. The fucking bastard would die. Rafe ached to get his hands on him and prayed at the same time that Emily would be okay.

"Holy shit!" One of the other officers who'd entered the house with them staggered backward into the living room, one hand over his mouth, while he pointed toward something with his other hand.

Without notice he ran to the front door, gagging as if he'd vomit. Tangari and Rafe raced toward the room the officer had just left.

"Oh God," Tangari said, years in the service being the only thing that kept him from puking at the sight of the woman on the bed.

"That explains the smell." Rafe's stomach turned, and he flipped on the light switch even though he didn't wear gloves. "Think you can expedite that search warrant?"

Tangari was already on his phone. "Any idea who she is?"

Rafe had a sinking idea who she was. And if he was right, and the dead woman with flies swarming around her was Beaux's wife, then it shot his theory clean out of the water as to who their murderer was.

Needing fresh air, needing to clear his head, Rafe stormed out of the house, heading for his car. Professionals would come in and sweep through the house with a fine-tooth comb. His job wasn't here. Right now all that mattered was finding Emily.

"Where are you going?" Tangari was on his ass.

"Emily's not here." Rafe jumped into his car, firing it up immediately.

"No shit. You didn't answer my question."

"They've got a thirty-minute lead on us." Rafe pulled his door shut and then rolled down his window. "But I've got a hunch. If he didn't think he was safe at his own home, maybe he took Emily to her house."

"You aren't going to break every law in the book to get over there." Again Tangari was on his phone. Barking orders, he pulled the phone from his ear a moment later. "What's her address?"

Rafe gave it to him and then Tangari assured him there would be a car at her apartment within minutes.

"I can't just sit here. Right now, I'm just in the way." Rafe put the car into gear. "Call me and I'll do the same if I find her."

It was all he could do not to push his car to the limit. Having so much power underneath him and fighting to do the speed limit was almost more than he could handle at the moment.

He wouldn't be able to live with himself if something happened to Emily. Knowing her for only a month, she'd brought something into his life that had been missing. Rafe knew he'd closed his heart off to the world. He'd quit living and hadn't realized it. Emily's craving for life, for adventure, her willingness to take on everything around her and give it her all, had brought back something in him that had almost died.

Gripping his steering wheel, he let go and then ran his fingers over it, trying to focus on traffic while an unfamiliar sensation rushed through him. His eyes burned. His heart hurt as if it would split in two. Every muscle in his body tensed.

Images of the dead women he'd found since the new school semester had started, and the women they'd discovered over the past year, floated through his mind, turning his stomach into knots.

That would not happen to Emily!

He almost attacked his phone when it rang. "What?" he barked.

"I got an officer reporting voices inside Emily's apartment." Tangari's words rushed through him, depleting all air from his lungs. "No one is answering the door. He just called for back up."

Energy rushed through him that he couldn't control. Hitting the accelerator hard with his foot, he dared any cop in the city to pull him over as he cut into the left lane and gunned it, heading for her exit.

"She better be fucking okay."

"Don't kill yourself getting there."

The back end of the Firebird swerved when Rafe cut into her parking lot and then skidded to a stop behind several squad cars. Barely taking time to slam the thing into neutral, he yanked up the parking brake and jumped out of the car. He was right behind the officers when they forced her apartment door open, guns drawn. Paying little attention to the suits, letting them do their job and get the scum out of her place, he saw only Emily's terrified expression turn to intense relief when she saw him.

"Rafe." She said his name on a sigh as she collapsed into his arms, shaking and wrapping her arms around him like she'd never let go.

Burying his head in her hair, he ran his arms down her back, pulling her closer, inhaling her scent.

"God. Babe." He couldn't find the words he wanted to say.

"I've never been more scared," she said, pulling back far enough to look up at him. "But we caught them. His mom did it."

Emotions attacked him too hard to reprimand her. Now that she was safe, in his arms where she belonged, he vowed silently that he'd do whatever it took to keep her there. Stroking her hair, he stared into her tear-stained face, seeing the glow in her eyes and the smile on her face.

"Well, I'm glad you've solved the case, Investigator, but as of this moment, you're retired."

Her grin broadened. "Only if you retire with me."

He shook his head, wanting to bend her over his knee, and pull her into his arms again and never let go.

"I hate to interrupt this reunion." Tangari walked up to them. "But I'm going to need you two down at the station."

Several hours later, after intensive questioning, and listening to recorded conversations from both Beaux and his mother, Molly Robinson, Rafe watched Emily sit in the chair next to him, her knee pulled up to her chin.

"I almost feel sorry for Beaux," she said quietly.

Joe Simpson, head of homicide, leaned back in his chair and crossed his arms. "Our psychiatrist got out of him that he'd witnessed his mother kill his father after catching him with an older woman."

"And it made her insane," Emily said.

The small TV in his office still showed the interview going on between the psychiatrist and Beaux. For a grown man, all appearances showing a jock who should have a promising future, he looked like a small child, rocking back and forth and crying as he looked around him nervously.

Rafe had a hard time feeling sorry for him. There were many people out there who grew up with messed-up parents. Some of them made it. Some of them didn't. But Beaux had gone after Rafe's woman. Thankfully, the cops had reached her apartment shortly after the Robinsons had gotten there. They'd interrupted the scene before Emily had been hurt or raped. If Beaux had touched her, Rafe would have killed him.

"When we interviewed her, she repeatedly got names confused. She's been living that scene of catching her husband with another woman over and over for years."

"And she used Beaux to keep the scene alive. I'm just glad it's over, for both of them." Emily looked at him, her large breast smashed against her knee. "Can we go now? I really need a change of scenery."

He was more than willing to get her out of there.

After showers and a change of clothes, Emily walked into his kitchen, barefoot with her hair damp around her face. All she wore was one of his large T-shirts, and he'd never seen a woman look sexier.

"I don't have any more clothes over here." She shrugged when she saw him take in her attire.

There was no way he could keep his hands off her. Reaching for a nipple, he tugged on it, pulling her closer.

"We need to do something about that."

"About what?" She ran her hands over his bare chest, sending heat rushing through him.

His cock hardened instantly. Rubbing her nipple between his thumb and finger, he ran his other hand through her hair. She let her head fall back, relaxing against his grip when he tangled his fingers in her wet hair.

"About your clothes being at the wrong house," he said, and then nipped at her lip when she would have commented.

She sighed into him, and he pulled her against him, wrapping his arms around her while their tongues explored each other's mouths. She tasted of toothpaste. And she opened so easily to him, submitting when he deepened the kiss.

She traced her fingers down his chest, brushing over his stomach and then grabbing the drawstring waistband of his sweatpants. A growl tore through him when she tugged at it and then pushed her hand lower until her fingers wrapped around his cock. All blood drained straight from his head, stealing his breath as his cock swelled, pulsing eagerly from her touch.

"Damn. Woman." He dragged his tongue over her cheek, nipping at her neck.

"I need you now," she whispered.

He had no problem with that.

Grabbing her shirt, he tugged it over her body. She moaned and lifted her arms, her body appearing before him, stretched and fucking perfect when he stripped the material that blocked his view out of the way.

She shoved at his sweats, pushing them down his thighs and then moving to her knees in front of him as she pushed them down his legs. He stepped out of them and then put his hands on her head, keeping her there, right where he wanted her. His cock throbbed with an energy he feared he couldn't control. Her breath against him was more torture than he could endure.

"God. Damn." He closed his eyes, fighting not to slam his cock down her throat when she sucked him into her mouth. "That is so damned good."

She hummed, and the vibration went through his cock. He grew in her mouth, hardening painfully, his muscles clenched as he did his best to let her control the act. More than anything he wanted to fuck her hard and fast.

And she wasn't making it easy on him. Emily took him on with an energy that left him dizzy. Sucking him deep into her moist heat, her tongue danced around his shaft while her soft lips about made him explode.

"Get your ass up here," he growled, letting go of her head and grabbing her arms quickly, before he pounded her harder than he knew she would be able to handle.

She looked up at him, her eyes and lips moist, and grinned. "So demanding," she purred, seeming quite delighted with herself that she'd almost sent him over the edge.

"I'll show you demanding," he said through clenched teeth and pulled her up quickly.

Turning her around and pushing her down against his counter, he grabbed his cock, pushing it toward her eager pussy.

She shook her ass, making him work to thrust into her soaked cunt. He gripped her ass, holding her still, and slammed inside her.

"Oh fuck yeah," she cried out, arching her back.

Her damp auburn hair clung to her narrow back. He watched his cock disappear into her tight pussy, his vision blurring as her heat rushed through him. Never had anything felt better in all of his life. And it took more than he had to keep the motion slow, enjoying how her muscles clamped around him.

"Faster, damn it. God. Please." She looked over her shoulder, reaching one hand behind her, as if she could make him go faster and somehow control the situation.

"You'll get what you need," he told her, fighting not to give in, wanting just a few more minutes to enjoy how she soaked him.

"Rafe," she begged.

Everything inside him shattered when she said his name. He buried himself deep inside her and then gripped her ass harder as he let her have what she wanted. Pounding her cunt, she screamed as he fucked her with enough momentum that fire burned from his cock, flaring inside him, burning him alive. Both of her hands quickly gripped the counter and she arched her back further, doing her best to move her ass, drive him mad with her teasing efforts.

Pressure burned through him. Every muscle in his body hardened while everything he had drained deep into her. She cried out, her pussy muscles clamping down so hard on him he thought she'd suffocate the life right out of him.

"Yes." She collapsed onto the counter, breathing so hard he wondered if he'd hurt her.

Bending over her, he gently kissed her back and she made a cooing sound that sent shivers through his cock.

"Rafe," she said quietly. "I…"

She paused, and his heart started beating too fast. Never had such a warmth rushed through him like it did now.

He slid out of her with deliberate slowness, his cock immediately craving the warm place where it had just been. Taking her shoulders, he pulled her to him, turning her around. Instead of looking at him, she buried her head in his chest.

His fingers tingled with energy still rushing through him. Running his hand down the side of her head, he cupped her chin.

"Emily," he said quietly, searching her expression as he lifted her face so he could see her. "Open your eyes."

She blinked and then stared up at him.

"What did you mean?" she began, and then bit her lip. She searched his face, sudden turmoil making her cheeks flush. "What did you mean when you said my clothes were at the wrong house?"

"I need you, Emily." He would say what she was afraid to say. "I love you, damn it. Woman. You're mine."

A broken sigh escaped her lips and her mouth parted. For a moment she didn't say anything and then she cleared her voice, looking down.

"Rafe. I love you too," she whispered and then buried her face in his chest.

He held her, resting his chin on her head. A peace rushed through him that he knew he'd never experienced before. Emily was his perfect match. Her wild side would challenge him, but he knew no other man would be able to handle her.

"Damn good thing," he told her, tightening his grip around her.

She chuckled but made no attempt to move. "Yup. Damn good thing," she said, and he knew she was smiling.

Enjoy an excerpt from:
CAUGHT!

Copyright © Lorie O'Clare, 2005.

She let her gaze fall out of focus as she stared through the blurred glass into the darkness and watched Jordan disappear. A flash of lightning, followed by a quick clap of thunder, brought her to attention, and she grew aware of every sound around her.

Roxanne turned quickly when a tapping noise sounded, only to scan the empty lobby cast with long shadows. She surveyed the large open area, her surroundings familiar. Well waxed tiles on the floor glistened with every flash of lightning, and the high ceiling made the thunder echo. With a sigh, she turned to face the doors and wait. Once again tapping sounded behind her, and she turned again, almost tripping over her own toes.

"Would you quit it," she scowled to herself. "It's nothing but pipes."

The sound of her own voice calmed her a bit, but her senses remained heightened, and every minute sound alerted her. She felt on edge, and blamed it on lack of sleep. The tapping sounded again, but she refused to turn this time, although prickles down her spine made her anxious to leave. Maybe she should just wait for Jordan outside.

Roxanne pushed the handle to open the glass door. Damp air surrounded her, and at the same time she felt the toes of her pantyhose saturate with water. Rain hit her arms and soaked through the material of her dress. She hadn't taken more than a step when headlights approached her. Roxanne frowned when she recognized Jordan's tan Porsche, instead of her own Probe. Why the hell had he taken her keys if it wasn't to bring her car to her?

"Why are you standing in the rain?" Jordan exited his car and walked around, then took her arm. He slid his card through the security box, pressed the necessary buttons and escorted her back into the building. "Look at you. You're soaked."

"I thought you were bringing my car to me." Roxanne wiped rain from her face with her free hand, since she was unable to release her other arm from Jordan's grasp. Her chin length bangs that she had been trying to grow out forever it seemed, stuck to her cheek, and she brushed them aside. Her mood turned sour as she realized she must look a wreck now in front of Jordan, who, although a bit damp, still looked sexy as hell.

"I'm going to take you to dinner." Jordan released her and stood appraising her. "But now we need to clean you up. What possessed you to stand outside?"

Roxanne felt foolish and frustrated at the same time. It was just like Jordan to assume she would want to go to dinner with him. She had planned on taking herself home to a hot bath. Her emotions laced with aggravation at his pompous attitude, and a sense of excitement that he had thought to reward her hard work by taking her to dinner.

"I heard something," she mumbled, doing her best to dry herself with her hand.

Jordan didn't respond, and the silence grew between the two of them. Roxanne decided her actions didn't require justifying, and straightened.

"Why did you ask for the keys to my car, and then not bring it to me?"

After all, her work day had ended, and now Jordan Hall was just a man, not her boss. She felt a tremble when she met his gaze, and narrowed her lips into a thin line, feeling herself grow wet, knowing she would submit to him if she didn't stand her ground. "And why would you assume I would go to dinner with you?"

"I would never leave you anywhere if you weren't safe." Jordan spoke quietly, almost a whisper, sounding so calm she blinked, momentarily forgetting her guard. "We need to get you dry before we go eat."

She licked her lips and wondered what it would be like to kiss this virile man. At the same time she realized he hadn't answered her question. She didn't need him thinking for her.

Jordan turned, putting his hand on the back of her head, and guided them back to the elevator. His hand slid from her head to between her shoulder blades, and remained there until the doors opened on the seventh floor. Roxanne felt certain her dress dried on her backside just from the heat of his touch.

"I can dry myself in the bathroom." Roxanne slowed when they reached the bathrooms, but Jordan's fingers pressed into her skin on her back, angling her beyond the restroom doors.

They walked silently to his office, and then Jordan took her arms and backed her up against his desk, so that her rear end rested on the edge.

"I want to dry you off." Jordan placed his index finger under her chin, lifting her head so that he could meet her gaze. "You need to trust me."

Overwhelming domination swirled in those black eyes, captivating her.

She laughed, trying to make light of the situation that had her pussy throbbing. "I've never had a reason not to trust you. But I'm quite capable of drying myself off."

Jordan turned as if he hadn't heard her, slipping his overcoat onto the chair, and then opening the cabinets next to the sink.

Roxanne remained glued to the edge of his desk, allowing herself an eyeful of the man while his back was turned. She should walk out of the office. The bathroom was the safest place for her to put herself back in order. But damn, did he make it hard for her to just walk out on him.

His white shirt spread over a broad, muscular back, and then narrowed into his work slacks, which covered what she was sure had to be the perfect male ass. Jordan turned at that moment, and with her eyes set at the level of his ass, she found she now saw a bulge through his pants. She wondered, while quickly averting her gaze, if the fullness she had noticed was due to the pleats in the slacks, or if he was simply very well-endowed.

"Hold out your arms." Jordan returned to stand in front of her with several white towels in his hands. He leaned into her slightly, placing two towels on the desk next to her, then unfolded the one he still held.

She raised her arms, her heart pounding. Jordan never offered explanations with his instructions. But his instructions had never been on such a personal level before.

"Like this." Jordan took one of her wrists and stretched her arm so that it straightened parallel to her shoulder. She did the same with her other arm, her heartbeat pulsing in her pussy lips, distracting her while it swelled and moistened.

Jordan began towel-drying her arms, caressing them gently with the towel. "The rain soaked you, didn't it?"

The roughness of the small towel sent chills rushing through her. And she didn't answer right away.

Jordan met her gaze, stroking her skin with small movements. Those black eyes captured her, captivated her, and she didn't look away. Barely able to breathe, pressure built, making her ache for him.

Why an electronic book?

We live in the Information Age — an exciting time in the history of human civilization, in which technology rules supreme and continues to progress in leaps and bounds every minute of every day. For a multitude of reasons, more and more avid literary fans are opting to purchase e-books instead of paper books. The question from those not yet initiated into the world of electronic reading is simply: *Why?*

1. *Price.* An electronic title at Ellora's Cave Publishing and Cerridwen Press runs anywhere from 40% to 75% less than the cover price of the exact same title in paperback format. Why? Basic mathematics and cost. It is less expensive to publish an e-book (no paper and printing, no warehousing and shipping) than it is to publish a paperback, so the savings are passed along to the consumer.

2. *Space.* Running out of room in your house for your books? That is one worry you will never have with electronic books. For a low one-time cost, you can purchase a handheld device specifically designed for e-reading. Many e-readers have large, convenient screens for viewing. Better yet, hundreds of titles can be stored within your new library — on a single microchip. There are a variety of e-readers from different manufacturers. You can also read e-books on your PC or laptop computer. (Please note that Ellora's Cave does not endorse any specific brands.

You can check our websites at www.ellorascave.com or www.cerridwenpress.com for information we make available to new consumers.)

3. *Mobility.* Because your new e-library consists of only a microchip within a small, easily transportable e-reader, your entire cache of books can be taken with you wherever you go.

4. *Personal Viewing Preferences.* Are the words you are currently reading too small? Too large? Too... ANNOYING? Paperback books cannot be modified according to personal preferences, but e-books can.

5. *Instant Gratification.* Is it the middle of the night and all the bookstores near you are closed? Are you tired of waiting days, sometimes weeks, for bookstores to ship the novels you bought? Ellora's Cave Publishing sells instantaneous downloads twenty-four hours a day, seven days a week, every day of the year. Our webstore is never closed. Our e-book delivery system is 100% automated, meaning your order is filled as soon as you pay for it.

Those are a few of the top reasons why electronic books are replacing paperbacks for many avid readers.

As always, Ellora's Cave and Cerridwen Press welcome your questions and comments. We invite you to email us at Comments@ellorascave.com or write to us directly at Ellora's Cave Publishing Inc., 1056 Home Avenue, Akron, OH 44310-3502.

erridwen, the Celtic Goddess of wisdom, was the muse who brought inspiration to storytellers and those in the creative arts. Cerridwen Press encompasses the best and most innovative stories in all genres of today's fiction. Visit our site and discover the newest titles by talented authors who still get inspired - much like the ancient storytellers did, once upon a time.